Sarah's Lottery

by
Brent Harris

Acknowledgements:

Cover Photo by Sarah Mitchell

ISBN-13: 978-1478138648

*This story is dedicated
to everyone who ever disliked a story enough
to write an alternative.
This is my alternative.*

Contents

Chapter 1

Deep beneath a vale of darkness, evil slept. Like a lingering mist, it surrounded the village, penetrating into every open space. Nestled beneath tall mountains that appeared like shadows in the pale moonlight, great oak and willow trees kept still; their branches curled inward in submission to a secret evil. A river flowed silently by.

Well hidden in the center of the wooded valley, the village burned with an invisible flame. Small wooden homes and buildings surrounded an old meeting house in a circular fashion. The meeting house had outlived its use. Its cold interior, now lit by a bright, solitary computer screen, was the very heart of evil, the flame the village had submitted to long ago.

Sarah Mitchell knew all too well about the flame, for it had touched her life in a very tragic way. She sat in the old meeting house that night in an old, wooden chair, typing her story to the silence, hoping that someday someone would read about her past…

It was Friday, the last day of the week that Peter Snotgrasse would have to spend cooped up in his small office. A young woman with long red hair pushed through his office door and walked into the dimly lit room. "Here's your mail," she said with a soft voice and sat the rather large bundle on his desk.

"Already the thirteenth?" he replied with a growl.

The woman nodded. "You've got about an hour."

"Fine!" he snarled. "Make sure you are there."

The woman silently left the room.

Pete leaned forward in his brown leather chair, untied the rope that held the bundle of mail together and opened the top envelope. He laughed. "Those electric people are at it again. Just because the new ones spit ice and water out their front doors, that don't mean I have to recycle my old fridge!" He sat the envelope aside and opened the next one.

"I am the Mayor of Wachmikilu! I will not use any less water than what I am using now!" He slammed that envelope down on his desk and opened the next one on the stack.

"Finally, a new library card. That reminds me, I need to check out *Runes: The Power Behind Ancient Symbology*. I must remember to do that this evening." He put the card in his back pocket and opened another envelope.

"Coupons, don't need 'em, don't use 'em." He tore the contents and the envelope to shreds. The rest of the mail consisted of three letters from the village school, each one requesting some addition to the school building. One envelope contained a bill from the local hospital for a checkup he had received the past week. Once he had

2

opened every envelope, Pete made his way from his office to the old meeting house at the center of the village. It was there that the event, the Lottery, began.

The Lottery, the secret flame that would not be extinguished, was, like the name implied, a contest by which many participated, but only one won. But this was, though, not a contest anyone desired to participate. The participants, the villagers of Wachmikilu, always took part in the contest for as long as they could remember; it was part of the requirement for living in the village. No villager spoke of this contest to anyone, not even each other. The only time it was spoken of openly was on the day it was held.

The Lottery was held the first Friday the thirteenth of the year. The Lottery had strict rules. The participants were the residents of the village. Any resident not present at the Lottery was hunted down and killed. Non-residents who were present in the village on the day of the Lottery were automatically made residents and required to attend the event, although this rarely happened.

All non-residents outside the village on the day of the Lottery did not participate in the event. The mayor of Wachmikilu was the only living resident not bound to participate in the Lottery, but he must preside over it.

Was there a way to get out of participation in the Lottery once one became a resident of the village? The answer was yes, but it was almost unachievable. The person must possess the qualifications to become the next mayor. Was this by design or some twisted sense of torture for a single person? No one knew.

Sarah was only one month old when she participated in her first Lottery. There were no age limitations or age requirements; all residents participated.

It was mid afternoon. The whole village had gathered in the old meetinghouse. Peter Snotgrasse, known to the villagers as Dogleg Pete because of his bad leg, called the meeting to order behind a sturdy podium. His gruff voice echoed throughout the large main room in an eerie way. "Welcome, ladies and gentlemen of Wachmikilu, to another run of the Lottery! Let me also welcome those who may be visiting the village. By attending this event, it gives us great pleasure to welcome you as a part of our community. For those of you not wishing to participate in this year's event, please step outside and let one of our trained officials," Pete cleared his throat, "deal with you. Let us also honor the tradition of our forefathers and be thankful we are alive and here today." Pete turned towards a tall man who had not mingled with the others when they came in. "Joe, are there any visitors to our village today?"

Joe shook his head.

"Good. You all know that outsiders are bad. If they knew what went on here, they'd put a stop to our beloved run of the Lottery."

The mayor then pulled a small sack from inside the podium and began walking around the room. He approached the head of each family and handed them a wadded up cloth from the sack. Each one just stood there, motionless, holding their cloth in their closed hands. No one looked at their cloth or dared to open it up too soon.

Once the mayor had finished passing out the bundles, people started unfolding them, slowly. Great sighs of relief echoed as the heads of each household began holding up blank cloths. Then an "Oh no" was whispered. The words came from John Botmfeedhr. His family backed away as he opened the cloth bearing a dark center. The mayor approached John and began laughing when the cloth was fully open. The dark area was a grape juice stain obtained some years back when someone had used the cloth to clean up after a kids' party. His family began to sigh in relief.

Then a small stone flew through the air and bounced off John Botmfeedhr's chest. It was thrown by none other than Billy Thuderdyke, the village prankster. He came from a very wealthy family. He was spoiled and never disciplined by his parents. Peter stepped in between the two men as Billy's father began advancing and swinging his arms, preventing either man from harming the other.

"Now John, let's not do anything rash." Pete turned to face the youth. "Billy, this is a serious matter. You know better than to bring your jokes in here."

Pete then glanced around the room. No one had appeared to find the winning mark yet, and there were still a few men holding wadded up cloths in their shaking hands. Pete walked up to a tall man standing next to his wife, who was holding their infant daughter. "Why Doc, you haven't opened yours yet. What's wrong? You're usually one of the first to open their bundle."

Dr. Kyle Smith held up the bundled cloth. "I'm the best doctor you've got here. If I'm gone, this village is not going to last long."

Pete snickered. "It's ironic that you put it that way. Does one Lottery have the potential of doing in the entire village? Go ahead, open it up and see what you have there."

The good doctor had a bad feeling about the event ever since he had woken up that morning. Slowly he opened the cloth revealing a large, black spot in the middle. Time seemed to stop as the cloth floated to the floor.

Ladies all over the room cringed. If word got out that each one of them had at some point had a relationship with the good doctor, their lives would surely be in danger. Each one held their tongues and their complexions as they all realized the situation that was unfolding before them.

Dr. Smith then raised his hand to punch the mayor, but Pete grabbed his arm. The mayor forced the doctor's hand back so fast that he broke the doc's wrist. The mayor then said in a loud and low voice, "Run!"

Dr. Smith ran from the meetinghouse followed by his wife with their infant daughter held tightly in her arms. Mrs. Smith's parents and Dr. Smith's father followed them.

After a couple minutes, the rest of the villagers reached down, picked up their large sacks and threw them over their shoulders. They marched out of the meetinghouse towards the way the Smiths had run.

"Hey, Abe, did you see the stranger in town yesterday?"

Abe, a grey haired gentleman with a jet black mustache pulled a baseball sized stone from his sack and began tossing it into the air as he walked. "Yep."

The shorter of the two men, bald and slightly over-weight, struggled to pull a rather large stone from his sack. "Did you talk to him?"

"Nope."

"Well, I did. He said his Gee-Pee-Something took him the wrong way. I'm guessing he wound up here by mistake."

"Did you ask him to stay the night?"

The shorter man froze. "You're joking, right? We don't need any more knowing about today."

"That's right, Frank," commented an energetic boy with red hair. "Them outsiders would come in and spoil all our fun. Where else can you get away with murder?"

The boy's wicked smile was matched by Abe's own smile. "Just wait till you're the one running."

Frank, Abe and the boy continued talking until they came to a stop.

The villagers had caught up with the grandparents. They were huddled under a tree, since none of them could run very fast or for very long. The villagers lined up, pulled large stones from their sacks, and executed the three elderly Smiths.

Not too far away, Abby Mitchell, a middle aged lady of the village with long red hair, darted from the shadow of one tree to another and came across Mrs. Smith. The doctor's wife was lying on the ground. She had been struck down as she was running. Abby deduced that she had been running with Dr. Smith and that the villagers had been aiming for him since the trail of stones kept on going. Abby then spotted a small bundle of white lying a few feet from Mrs. Smith. It was the infant. She quickly picked the infant up and pulled back the cloth that was lightly wrapped around her head. She saw two inquisitive blue eyes staring up at her, full of life.

Abby thought quickly. Using some medical knowledge she had gained from her time spent with Dr. Smith and some spare medicines she carried around with her, she sedated the infant into a deep sleep. She then tore some of the loose wrappings off and dabbed them against Mrs. Smith's open wounds. Throwing the loose pieces to the ground to give the impression that an animal had attacked, she removed some of the stones from her sack and carefully placed the infant inside. She closed up the sack with just enough room left to reach inside and grab another stone if she needed one. Then, picking up a stone from the ground, she headed off in the direction of the stone trail.

It was not long before she came across some of the villagers heading back her way. "I heard they ran this way," she called out to them as they approached. "Did you catch up with them?"

"Yes, we did," came the reply from one of the villagers. "The Doc did not go quietly or easily. Did you see his wife? We think she went down somewhere to the east of us."

Abby shook her head.

"We found Mrs. Smith," came a voice from behind Abby. More villagers came up from the southeast. "She was killed in the crossfire as you aimed for the Doc. We also found these." He held up a handful of torn cloth covered in blood. "Looks like the infant was taken off by some animal."

"Good," said the villager from the north. "What about the grandparents?"

"They were taken care of under the old willow to the west of us. Looks like this year's Lottery has come to a close. Let's all head back to the village."

That night, the bodies were gathered and buried. Meanwhile, Abby prepared to pay the mayor a visit on the following day.

The mayor looked up from his morning paper at the young woman with long, red hair. The breath from his large nostrils pushed aside the steam that rose from his ancient mug. His brow wrinkled. "She forgot the nutmeg, cinnamon, and brown sugar," he muttered under his breath. "Must be worried about finding a new doctor." His mood changed a little when he realized who had come to see him.

"I believe she's pre-occupied with sorting the morning mail."

"I thought that was your job."

"It was." Abby thought long and hard about what she was about to say. "I would like to request a termination of my residency here."

Dogleg pulled a pocketknife from a drawer in his desk and began to play with it. "That is a serious request. Are you sure?" he asked.

Abby nodded but knew deep down that if she was wrong, that the knife would do more than just dance between Pete's fingers. "Yes, I am sure."

The mayor stood and walked over to a dusty old bookshelf. He pulled a rather large old register from the shelf and set it onto his desk. He opened it up, flipped through the pages and began mumbling. "Margretts, Messyweather, Menymold, ah here it is, Mitchell. Hmmm. Grandparents are dead. Parents died two years ago. No children. Yes, it does look like you qualify for residency termination." He pulled out a document from his filing cabinet and handed it to Abby. "If you could sign and date this, I can let you be on your way."

Abby signed the document and left the mayor's office, almost tearing the door from its hinges as she burst through it to taste the fresh air of freedom! Within the next few hours, she had packed as much into her luggage as possible and rode away from the village in a large truck belonging to a visitor to the village. The lady had followed the old Route 99, which dead ended right into the village. There was only one way out of the village, south by means of this major highway. The lady accepted Abby's plea to take her to wherever she was headed.

Abby was glad to be leaving the village, glad to be leaving with her daughter, Sarah.

Chapter 2

Abby was dropped off with her daughter at the base of a brand new hospital in a big city. If it wasn't her charm and good looks that got her the job, it was certainly Sarah's. Abby's skill set landed her a nurse's assistant position, but she was a quick learner and became an LVN (Licensed Vocational Nurse) within the year.

She was given a two bedroom apartment to live in with Sarah. Night after night, Abby would fall asleep with Sarah in her arms while feeding her in the same purple, thickly padded, lounge chair. Then, like clockwork, Abby would wake up at midnight and put Sarah in her light pink crib, smile as Sarah turned onto her side and slid her thumb into her mouth, and quietly turn and climb into her own bed for the night. Morning would come floating in on the aroma of sweet Brazilian coffee.

It was on one particular morning that Sarah came dancing into the room with her bright pink backpack on, bright red hair swinging from side to side, and something red held in both hands.

"It's a puppy!" Sarah's face beamed as she handed the play dough sculpture to her mother. She had worked half the previous night away making it just right.

"It's beautiful," Abby replied back, taking the red glob, which for a young first grader, was a good resemblance to a real puppy.

When Abby had the unfortunate responsibility of informing her patients of bad news, it was Sarah's opportunity to make something special for those patients. Today, the elderly lady in room 5-G would get the news that her kidneys were failing and a red puppy.

"Look, Mom, I'm flying!" Steam surrounded Sarah as she floated around the room one day in middle school on her latest engineering project.

"Be sure not to go to high," replied her mother, even though Sarah was only inches off the floor.

High school was no different. Abby walked into her kitchen, hoping to find her favorite cup of coffee waiting for her, only to find that the kitchen had been transformed into a mad scientist's lair! Beakers of boiling liquid popped and hissed as clouds of white rolled from their tops around the counter tops. Sarah cackled as she dropped some pieces of her hair into one beaker with a thick black liquid and stirred it with a crystal tipped rod.

"You're not giving that to any of *my* patients."

Sarah laughed. "Don't worry, Mom, this one is for the school play." She picked up a beaker with blue liquid and handed it to Abby. "Here, the boy in room 3-B could use this for his cough. And this one," she held up a beaker with green liquid. "This one would be perfect for the girl in 3-F; it will ease the itching and pain from her burns."

12

Abby knew that it was time. Sarah had already excelled in her classes far above her classmates. She agreed to allow Sarah to enroll in some basic college classes by correspondence. By the time she graduated, they had paid off.

Sarah stood in her bathroom, oblivious to the low rumble of the traffic outside, combing her long, red hair that resembled Abby's hair. Her face, illuminated by the sunlight streaming in from the bathroom window, had matured quite well along with her bright blue eyes, short pointed nose, and a quiet smile.

"Sarah, are you ready for your first big day?"

"Yes. After those basic college classes you let me take, I'm ready for the work, but I'm not sure I'm ready to be so far away from home."

"I know," her Mom replied, placing a hand on her shoulder. "You'll be fine. Have you enjoyed the break in contests?"

"I love it! It's given me a lot of time to pack and get ready for college."

"Are you sure you want to continue them?"

"Of course! I need something to challenge my studies with. But, don't worry, Mom, I won't let them interfere with my grades."

"Good. Now come in here, I've got something for you."

Abby led Sarah into her bedroom where sat a large box on the bed. It was a laptop computer, and it was a nice one at that! Sarah threw her arms around her mother. "Thank you, Mom! I'm going to need that!"

Abby laughed. "You're welcome."

Sarah sat down on the bed and began to look over the outside of the box. "Now you can look at it, but let's wait until you get to the dorm before you open it."

Sarah sighed. "Okay, Mom."

Abby helped Sarah load her things into Abby's old van. The van was once an ambulance used by the hospital before they upgraded to newer models. Abby kept it loaded with supplies for non-official medical transportation to and from the hospital.

Abby and Sarah traveled the three and a half hour drive and arrived at Eagle Point University around noon. The first thing they did after arriving was to get checked in at the administration building. The lady took Sarah's picture and gave her an ID card, which allowed her to go to the campus cafeterias whenever she wanted. In fact, they headed over to the closest cafeteria next, for they were both very hungry.

The campus was setup to have everything a student would need without having to step outside the gates. The administration oversaw everything to do with governing the place from a three story building on the northern side of the campus. There was a social area near the wall of post office boxes in the one story building on the southern side of the campus. The classrooms were in towers that surrounded a grand, domed theater for special dramas located in the center of the campus. Three super-sized cafeterias stood in a triangle around these buildings so that no one would go hungry. Flanked on all corners were four magnificent towers that housed the students. To most, the campus looked like a small city.

After lunch, Abby and Sarah headed over to north east tower which was where Sarah would live. Abby was very glad that the dorms were not coed. Katie and Zammie Plier greeted Sarah at the door of her dorm room.

"Hello. I'm Sarah, and this is my mother."

"Hi, Sarah! I'm Katie, and this is my twin sister, Zammie. We're your roommates!"

Zammie nodded with a sheepish smile. "Hi."

"Need some help moving in your things?"

"Yes," replied Sarah, "that would be great."

Katie and Zammie helped move all of Sarah's things from the van to their dorm room on the third floor. They both got very excited when they saw her laptop box because they saw that she had not yet opened it. Sarah's mother insisted that Sarah wait until after she had left before opening it.

The room had its own restroom, large walk-in closet, four tall bookshelves, two sets of bunk beds, and a lot of open space in the center of the room for a couple of desks.

"We've ordered two custom desks," commented Zammie. "They are big enough for two people each."

"That's right. They should be here tomorrow. It's too bad that the university doesn't provide desks in every room. Thankfully, we got some chairs."

Sarah and her mother sat in the two chairs while Katie and Zammie took seats on their lower bunks. "Tell us a little about yourselves," Abby said to the two young ladies.

"Well, as I'm sure you noticed, we are twins." They were both tall and very slender. Katie had long, black hair while Zammie wore short, brown hair. Their hair was the key to telling them apart. "We are from up north where it's cold. This is our first year here. I am studying engineering with a minor in computer science, and Zammie is studying chemistry with a minor in computer science as well. We both want to be teachers."

"What about you?" Zammie asked Sarah.

"Well, I'm into all those subjects," replied Sarah. "But I'm going to just do two. How about I do engineering and chemistry? Then we could all share classes!"

"A double major! Wow! That's going to be tough."

"Well, Zammie, Sarah's no average girl," Abby added in.

"Tell us."

"Yeah, tell us," chimed in Zammie.

Sarah blushed, but Abby went right into describing Sarah's upbringing.

"Let me see, where to begin. I guess it all started shortly after I started working at the Mary Elizabeth Kikillian Memorial Hospital as an RN. I was fresh out of a five year nursing degree, and Sarah was just starting first grade. Her bus would drop her off after school at the hospital where she would stay there with me for an hour or two. She was fascinated with medicine.

"Her teachers would call me and tell me all about the wonderful masterpieces that she was making out of play dough. By the time she was in the second grade, she sculpted modeling clay into many get well gifts for the patients at the hospital. I still have many of the sculptures she made for me at my nurse's station today. She learned early the value of cheering others up.

"When she turned eleven, I gave her an engineering set. She loved it! Night and day, all I heard were beeps and whistles from the thing. By sixth grade, she was competing in engineering contests. Frequent winnings told me that I had better do something about them, so I opened up a savings account for her to keep the money in.

"When she was in the tenth grade, I rewarded her hard work with a chemistry set. After only a little coaching from me, she started preparing some very delicate medicines that astounded the druggists at the hospital. I am very proud of my girl! She graduated top of her class. Next thing we knew, we were here."

"Wow!" replied Katie. "I'm sure your father must be very proud!"

There was silence.

"I'm sorry, Katie. We don't speak of her father much. He passed away shortly after she was born."

There was more silence.

"Come on, girls, cheer up! You've got a great dorm room here, and you are about to start on some of the most wonderful years of your lives! Sarah, I need to be saying good-bye and head back. Do you have everything?"

Sarah nodded.

After saying good-bye to her mother, Sarah decided not to open her new laptop just yet. She knew it would consume the rest of her evening, and Katie and Zammie wanted to go to the mall, so Sarah joined them. They spent the next couple hours shopping for items for their dorm room. They were exhausted by the time they got back and were ready to relax and examine the new computer.

Chapter 3

One month had passed, and the three girls were heavily into their studies. The laptop proved to be a great help with Sarah's studies and papers. On Monday, Sarah had Chemistry 101 with Zammie. After class, Zammie came up to her and said, "Sarah, I'm struggling with the way this teacher is presenting the material. Could you help me?"

"Sure. Let's plan to do some studying after supper tonight in our room."

"Thank you! You know we got a test coming up on Wednesday. I want to be ready for it."

"Don't worry, Zammie, we both will be ready!"

That evening, the girls walked back to their dorm room discussing what they had planned for the evening.

"Zammie has asked for some help with her Chemistry class," Sarah said to the brisk evening air. She had seen Katie up ahead out of the corner of her eye.

"We've got a test coming up, and I want to be ready for it," chimed in Zammie, playing along, not seeing Katie.

"Good," replied Katie. "Then maybe when you are done, you can give me some help with my Engineering 101."

Zammie froze, grabbing her chest and breathing heavily. When she got her breath back, she looked up and glared at Katie. After a few moments, the girls all broke into laughter and headed to their room.

Sarah had Engineering 101 with Katie on Tuesdays. She was hoping Katie would ask for help seeing as how she was struggling a little as well.

Sarah had no problems explaining the subjects to her roommates that evening. They wondered how she knew the subjects as well as she did. Sarah told them all about the contests she had participated in throughout elementary school and high school.

"Could we participate with you in some of these contests?" Katie asked.

"I don't see why not," replied Sarah. "You will need to come up with some good experiments though."

"What is your next one going to be?" Zammie asked.

"I'm not quite sure yet. Let's get through this week's worth of work first. We can discuss some side projects on the weekend."

The weekend came and found the three girls studying hard in the library. Katie poured over an engineering book while Zammie looked through a chemistry book. Sarah found herself reading an engineering book and a chemistry book. Zammie was the first to come up with something. Her choice of projects was a volcano. Katie's project choice was a touch pad that could control the flow of power to several different devices. Sarah's project was a little more difficult, but she knew she could pull it off. It was a rocket bug that boosted itself to the ceiling and walked around waiting for someone to walk by. The bug would then squirt them with a jet of water.

Katie and Zammie came in second and third behind Sarah in the contest. This contest started a fun competition between the girls that would last for years to come. Only once did Sarah let the two sisters best her at a contest. It was in their second year.

"Congratulations, you finally beat me!" Sarah sneezed. "I guess instantly evaporating liquid isn't very popular any more."

"You were sick; you couldn't concentrate," replied Zammie. "Our robot doggy is nothing compared to the kind of things you come up with, even though it did eat food and poop into a little doggy bag."

"Thank you, Zammie."

"Now let's get back to the dorms, you need some sleep."

And with that, Katie and Zammie packed up the displays for themselves and Sarah, and the three girls headed back to the dorms.

Time passed, and the girls' third year was nearing completion. Sarah's contests allowed her to boost her work ethic and complete enough classes to achieve her double major in just three years. Finals were just around the corner, and it was not a time for Sarah to slack off.

Sarah sat in the Rhino Pit, a social gathering spot at the university, alone on a couch studying and writing an essay for her Advanced Alchemy class on the effects of combining various metals. Katie and Zammie sat close by at a round table writing their essays as well.

As Sarah was typing a particularly tough sentence, Josh plopped his athletic trim, basketball loving self down next to her. "Hello, Sarah, can't imagine what you are doing here..."

Josh was the captain of the Jokers, the university basketball team. He hung around with the Plier sisters and became attracted to Sarah. Being the nice girl that she was, Sarah didn't push him away, but she didn't fall to his charm either, and at this particular moment, he was an annoying sore that Sarah just wanted to go away.

"Hi, Josh. Well I know what you are NOT doing here." Sarah could only imagine what the basketball team's classes were like. Only doing the bare minimum to get a passing grade was Josh's motto. They were all the same on that team.

"Hey, Sarah, I just got this like cool new skateboard! It's like dead awesome!"

"That's nice..." Sarah didn't so much as turn her head but remained focused on her work.

"I'm mean... like... its super cool and all... listen. They put this wicked skull on the bottom with like the coolest looking diamonds as the eyes, and the teeth are like knives with blood dripping down and all that stuff."

"That's nice..." Again, Sarah's gaze did not stray from her computer screen.

"Sarah, don't you hear what I'm saying? Aren't you like freaked out and going to get upset with me for getting something so gruesome?"

"Yeah, sure. That's nice…"

Josh started to get upset. He moved his lips, but nothing came out. He frantically moved his hands in front of him trying to figure out what to do and say. This movement caught the eye of Katie. She tapped Zammie on the arm and whispered, "Something's not right. Look over at Josh." Zammie looked up from her work over at Josh. "Call Dexie. This will not end well."

Dexter Plier, brother of Katie and Zammie, always stayed a cell phone call away from his two younger sisters. Going through his senior year of a law degree, Dexter spent a great deal of time in the law books of the university library.

As Zammie was telling Dexter about the situation, Josh stood up and yelled, "Pay ME some attention sometime why don't ya!" He then grabbed Sarah's laptop from her lap and threw it across the room. It bounced off the wall and hit the floor causing various small components to burst from the case.

Zammie told her brother to hurry, and both girls stood and approached the scene. "Sit!" they both said in unison with fingers pointed in Josh's face.

Josh realized that his father would be very displeased with his actions, so he clammed up and sat back down.

The two girls looked over at Sarah and winked.

Sarah, who had not had enough time to react to what Josh had done, sat back and waited. Watching Katie and Zammie pace back and forth in front of her and Josh with such angry looks on their faces made Sarah forget that her laptop now sat broken next to the far wall.

Josh did not move nor make a sound.

With camera in hand, Dexter was ready for anything when he arrived at the Rhino Pit a few minutes later. He photographed the two on the couch, the two women who stood over them, the crowd of witnesses, and the laptop. He went around to the onlookers first, getting their account of what happened before approaching the scene.

Katie and Zammie were adamant about what they had seen and heard. In their mind, this "jock" did not deserve to be in their presence any longer, but they tolerated it so that some sense of justice might be served over his actions. Sarah's story matched perfectly with Katie and Zammie's account of what happened. Josh decided to remain silent and not comment on what he had done.

When Dexter had concluded his work, Katie and Zammie demanded that Josh leave the building. He did so. The two girls then helped Sarah pick up the pieces of her laptop and take them back to their dorm room.

Back in the dorm room, Sarah broke into tears.

"What a complete jerk! Am I right, Katie?"

"Right, Zammie! He's going to get it from Dexter, you just wait and see."

"What do you mean, Katie?" asked Sarah.

"Dexie's big senior project is to participate in a court hearing. This is going to be great! Josh won't know what hit him! I bet Dex will be the prosecuting attorney."

"You'll be the plaintiff," chimed in Zammie.

Sarah, who was lying down in her bed, turned to face the wall.

"Ok, Zammie, let's let her get some sleep."

The two girls let Sarah get to sleep. They, though, spent the rest of the evening pouring over Sarah's broken computer. They determined that all was lost except for the hard drive and were able to recover all of her important files.

Sarah went through the next day in a daze. The classes she shared with Katie and Zammie were a blur. She was counting on the notes that the other two took. It took a couple days before she was back into the swing of things. The university also lent her a new laptop to use until things could be settled.

Chapter 4

The gavel rang twice to a packed courtroom. The university had the courtroom built for this very purpose, to train young lawyers and courtroom students with a mock case. Sometimes, though, the students would try a real case, as in this situation. Both parties have agreed to abide by the arbitration of the judge.

Students filled the viewing seats while members of the community filled the jury. Sarah sat next to Dexter at the prosecution's table while Josh sat next to Jacob Thuderdyke, Josh's brother, at the defendant table.

"It's my pleasure to welcome you to another student courtroom case," proclaimed the judge, a tall, slender female judge with long black hair and a scowl to kill a horse. "For most of the students here, this is their final project here at Eagle Point University. For those students in attendance as spectators, take note; you'll be participating in your own trial in your upcoming years.

"Dexter Plier, it's good to see you in that seat. I know you've been waiting and working hard to get there.

I expect nothing less than your best here in this trial. I'm sure your sisters will have your hide if you do any less."

Katie and Zammie, both sitting directly behind Dexter, each put a hand on one of his shoulders. Katie whispered into his ear, "You know we will."

"And Jacob Thuderdyke," the judge continued, "you've managed to get high grades up to this point. I'm interested in seeing how you prove yourself in this case. Just like with your grades, money will not help you win.

"Dexter, let's begin with your opening statements."

"Thank you, your Honor." Dexter stood and addressed the jury. "Ladies and gentlemen of the jury, the case put before you involves the young man, Josh Thuderdyke, who desperately wanted the attention of the defendant, Sarah Mitchell. In his frustration and rage, Josh was seen throwing Sarah's laptop computer across the room, and damaging it beyond repair as it hit the wall.

"Josh was, without question, out of control and should be held financially responsible for his actions." Dexter walked back to his seat.

"Thank you, Dexter," replied the judge. She turned to Josh and his defense attorney. Jacob just sat there, looking at his notes. "Mr. Thuderdyke, do you have any opening statements?"

Jacob shook his head. "No, we do not."

"Very well then. Dexter, you may call your first witness."

"Thank you, your Honor. I call Tiffany White to the stand."

A tall, slender lady with dark skin and predominant features walked to the stand. The bailiff swore her in, and she took the seat.

"Miss White, tell us, if you will, where you were on the night in question."

"Why I was at the Rhino's Pit waiting on my good friend Clara Bell." Tiffany had a distinctly south-eastern accent. "We needed to plan what we were going to cook for our Sunday school class. We always make a large breakfast for them."

"How did it turn out?"

"Mmmm mmmm! It was the best steak and egg plate that Clara Bell has ever made! I got seconds."

"I will have to try it. Continuing on, what happened next at the Rhino Pit?"

"Well now, I was lookin' through my cook books when I heard someone yell. I looked up to find that boy," she pointed to Josh, "yelling at that young lady," she pointed to Sarah.

"Let the record reflect the witness pointed to Josh Thuderdyke first and then pointed to Sarah Mitchell second. Please continue, Miss Whtie."

"He then grabbed her computer and threw it across the room! It exploded into a thousand pieces! I was about to give that boy a talkin' to, but those Plier sisters beat me to it."

"What do you mean, 'beat you to it'?"

"They shut him up! First time anyone had stood up to him I figured. He did not look very happy."

"Thank you, Miss White." Dexter sat down.

Jacob stood to his feet. "Miss White, do you wear glasses?"

"Why yes I do, but just for reading."

"Were you wearing your glasses on the night in question?"

"Yes."

"Are you sure you could see the defendant, Josh Thuderdyke, clearly?

"Young man, I can see quite clearly over the tops of my glasses."

"Thank you, nothing further." Jacob sat back down.

The judge looked down at Tiffany. "Okay, Miss White, you may step down. Dexter, call your next witness."

"I call Mark Windhill to the stand."

A young man wearing thick glasses, a brown plaid shirt, and kaki pants walked slowly to the stand. After being sworn in, Dexter started with his questioning.

"Mark, where were you on the night in question?"

"At the Rhino Pit."

"And what, may I ask, were you doing?"

"Sleeping."

"Sleeping?"

"Yes, sleeping. I fell asleep doing my research project for Advanced 3D Gaming and Graphics." Mark looked over at Josh. "And I would have had a nice long nap until that jerk over there woke me up!"

"Okay, Mr. Windhill, let's calm down and tell me what happened."

"He grabbed that girl's laptop and threw it across the room."

"And then what happened?"

"I left and went back to my room to get some sleep."

"Thank you. No further questions."

Dexter took his seat, and Jacob stood up. "Tell me, Mr. Windhill, what woke you up, Josh yelling or the laptop hitting the wall?"

"That jerk's yelling."

"Are you sure? Think carefully. Wasn't it the laptop hitting the wall that woke you? If you didn't see who threw the laptop, how do you know it was Josh?"

"The dude was standing up! Sarah couldn't have thrown that laptop across the room while sitting down."

"Really… No more questions your Honor."

Dexter did not get any more verbal prompting from the judge; he took the nod in his direction as the indication to call his next witness. "I call Zammie Plier to the stand."

Zammie was sworn in and took her seat.

"Hello, Zammie."

"Hi, Dex."

"Could you tell us what happened on the night in question?"

"Yes. Sarah was working on a pretty tough assignment, and Katie and I were working on our own projects. I was surprised when Katie tapped me on the shoulder and pointed at Josh. He was moving his hands, well, like this." She imitated the wild, wavy movement for the court with her hands.

"What happened next?"

"He stood up and yelled at Sarah. The next thing we knew, Josh had grabbed Sarah's laptop and thrown it across the room! Katie and I had enough. We walked over to them and told him to sit down."

"Thank you, Zammie."

Jacob stood and approached the witness stand.

"Miss Plier, do you like Josh?"

Zammie shook her head.

"Oh? Why's that?"

"He's rude," replied Zammie.

"Right. And I'm sure you'd like to see him pay."

"No!"

"Now, Miss Plier, have you at any time seen Sarah Mitchell hit her computer?"

"N-N-No."

"You're hesitating. Have you seen her hit her computer?"

"Well, I've seen her," she paused, "pat the side of her computer. But..." Jacob cut her off.

"Thank you. No more questions."

Zammie gave Dexter a pleading look.

"Your Honor, permission to redirect the witness."

"Permission granted."

Dexter stood. "Zammie, why did Sarah hit her computer? Was it because she no longer liked her computer?"

Zammie shook her head and smiled; she was glad Dexter had given her the chance to finish her answer. "No, she occasionally got frustrated with the magnitude of her work load. It takes a special mind to do the amount research she does. She would never do anything to that computer nor would she ever get rid of it."

"Why's that?"

"That computer was special to her. It was given to her by her mother when she first came to Eagle Point. It meant a lot to her."

"Thank you, Zammie."

Dexter took his seat, and Zammie stepped down.

"I call Sarah Mitchell to the stand."

Sarah had been prepared for this.

"Sarah, we've heard from a couple people about what happened that night. Please tell us, in your own words, what happened."

"It all started when I decided to go to the Rhino Pit to finish some research on a particularly tough assignment. I was joined by Josh, who appeared to want to talk. I didn't have the time to get into a conversation, so I just let him talk.

"The next thing I knew, Josh was grabbing my laptop and throwing it across the room. I didn't even have time to respond when my good friends Katie and Zammie rushed over and told Josh to sit down.

"I sat there and waited."

"Thank you, Sarah." Dexter turned to the jury. "Sometimes the truth is a simple mater." In a fluid and planned manner, Dexter completed his turn and took his seat.

Jacob stood and approached.

"Sarah, I've heard that you've been having problems with your laptop. Is that correct?"

"No, the laptop was working perfectly."

Jacob faced the jury. "That's odd, people don't usually hit their computers unless something is not working right. Maybe you were frustrated with your research, I'm not sure, but tell the court who it really was who threw the laptop." He turned to face Sarah and pointed his finger at her. "Admit the court that it was you who threw the laptop!"

"No, I did not throw the laptop."

"No further questions." Jacob sat down.

The judge turned to Sarah. "You may step down."

Sarah took her seat by Dexter.

The judge looked down at Dexter who sat there, silent. "Mr. Plier, do you have any more witnesses?"

"Your Honor, the prosecution is ready to rest its case."

The judge turned to Jacob. "Mr. Thuderdyke, do you have any witnesses to call?"

"No, your honor, the defense rests."

The judge turned to face the jury. "You have heard the case presented before you today. You are released to deliberate. This court is in recess until deliberations are over."

The gavel rang.

Fifteen minutes later, the jury deliberations were completed, and everyone was back in the court room for the decision.

"Has the jury reached a verdict?"

"Yes, your Honor, we have. In the case of Mitchell vs. Thuderdyke, we the jury find the defendant, Josh Thuderdyke, guilty."

"Thank you, members of the jury. With the defendant being found guilty, it is the judgment of this court that he pay a predetermined sum of three-thousand dollars to Miss Mitchell for the purchase of a new computer to replace the one he damaged.

"Sarah, I am sorry you had to be dragged through this unfortunate event. I cannot replace a memory, but I know it is possible to create new ones. Josh, I hope that you have learned that anger will get you no where. It can even get you into lots of trouble.

"Dexter, well done and congratulations on your win. Jacob, meet me in my office in half an hour, we need to talk. All other students involved in this case, I commend you for a good job done. You will be receiving high scores for this final project."

The gavel rang for the last time, and the case was over.

Sarah gave Katie and Zammie hugs and thanked Dexter for his fine work.

It didn't take long for Sarah to pick out and configure the perfect laptop. Katie and Zammie used some of their earnings from contests to engrave the laptop with a tech savvy poem and also to get a laptop case and various accessories. The computer quickly became a tool of fun, entertainment and necessity.

Chapter 5

Dexter graduated that year at the top of his class, as did Sarah. Dexter took the girls out to eat on his graduation night and told them that he had been offered a position at a local law firm. He was very excited about taking the job and also about being able to stick around as his two sisters finished their degrees.

Sarah didn't celebrate her graduation much; she turned her focus to doing a third degree, computer science, and quickly enrolled for another year.

Sarah let her class load decrease that year and increased her attendance in contests, but Katie and Zammie had their class loads increase heavily since they were taking their final classes for graduation. Sarah helped them as much as she could.

The help paid off, and Katie and Zammie obtained their degrees. They were joined by Sarah and Dexter on their graduation night for supper. At the table, talk rose up about what they were going to do next.

"We've decided to stay around and become teachers at the Eagle Point Academy," replied Katie when Dexter posed the question about what they were going to do with their degrees.

Eagle Point Academy was a kindergarten through twelfth grade school started by graduates from Eagle Point University. Katie and Zammie had eaten lunch at the academy on several occasions and had grown fond of many of the students.

"They've already been accepted," commented Sarah. Sarah turned to the two sisters. "And I've got an ultra-crazy idea for the two of you. How would the two of you like to come and live with me in a mansion?"

"What? Where?" asked Zammie. "I don't remember seeing any mansions around here."

"That's because there aren't any; we are going to build one. I purchased a four acre plot of land five miles from the university. You know, over by the old windmill."

"Wow, a mansion! Sure we'd like to come and live with you there!" Katie was in complete agreement with her sister. "But how are we going to build it?"

"Let's wait and discuss that later," Sarah answered.

After hearing that, Katie and Zammie rushed through the rest of their food in an attempt to get out of the restaurant sooner.

Back in the girls' dorm room, Sarah started up a blueprint program on her laptop to go over the plans for the mansion. She was glad Katie and Zammie still had a couple days before they were required to move out of the dorm and into staff housing.

"So, how do we want to build this mansion?"

The excitement and anticipation were so great that the girls fell silent.

Sarah broke the silence. "Let's start with the basement."

"Bomb shelter. Let's make it like a bomb shelter."

"Interesting idea, Zammie. If we go that route, I'm seeing a room for sleeping, a room for living and a place for food storage."

"Bathroom. If it's going to be lived in, it's got to have at least one bathroom."

"Good one, Zammie, we can't forget about those! We'll put at least one bathroom on each floor."

"And a vault," added Katie, "we've got to have some place to store some extra money. And let's also put a computer room down there as well. It will be cool and safe."

"I like that." Zammie spoke with a little laugh. "I also want some tunnels and crawlways, you know, to get from room to room. I want it to be a fun place to go to."

"Those are great ideas!" Sarah took note of every one of them in her computer. "Now let's move on to the first floor."

"Kitchen," chimed in Zammie.

"Labs," added Katie. "We need space for our experiments and class work, not to mention our contests."

"How about a large foyer with a carpeted, spiral staircase leading up to the upper floors?" asked Sarah. Both of the other girls cheered the suggestion.

"Secret passages and doors and panels and stuff," added Zammie, "we've just got to have some hidden and secret things in our mansion."

The girls laughed. "Okay, Zammie, I'll see what I can do. Maybe I can put in a secret passage from the first floor to the computer room in the basement." Zammie nodded. "Let's move on to the second floor."

"Storage," commented Katie. "Let's use the second floor to store all of the things we don't use on a daily basis."

"I like that idea, Katie. Do we have any more thoughts on the second floor?"

Katie and Zammie shook their heads.

"Okay, what are we going to put on the third floor?"

"Bedrooms!" Katie cheered. "Grand bedrooms like the ones in fancy hotels!"

"And a dorm room," added Zammie, "we must have a dorm room like the ones here. For fun."

The girls laughed again.

"Let's not forget our own bathroom. We each need a private bathroom all to ourselves."

"Noted." Sarah continued to laugh. "Grand bedrooms have to have grand bathrooms! I say we put our bedrooms in the east wing and put some guest bedrooms in the west wing."

"Good idea, Sarah," Katie added. "Let's finish off the mansion with a fourth floor dedicated to our hobbies. We'll have rooms for crafting, sewing, and any other workshop we might need. I can also see small theater up there as well. Access to that floor will be by stairs at either end of the East and West wings."

"Perfect!" Zammie said with a cheer. "But how are we going to fund such a venture?"

"My contest winnings over the years have given me a rather large bank account. My mom also invested in some stocks when I was young, and they are about to mature. This should be enough without having to ask either of you to put any funds into this."

"Sarah, that's very nice of you, but we would love to put some of our funds into this, especially if we are going to live here too. I'm sure we've got enough, but let's make sure." Katie pulled a highly colorful brochure from her side bag and handed it to Sarah.

"Scientific America's Annual Tech Contest? I've been reading about that contest for years. You really think we have a chance?"

"You have a chance, Sarah, not us."

"Look, the grand prize is to have your product manufactured and sold by Scientific America itself! The first place prize is one million dollars! Even if you don't get either of those, a couple hundred thousand dollars from the lower prize levels will ensure that this place of ours gets built."

"Come on, Sarah, at least give it a try."

"Okay, you two, I'll give it a shot. What do you suggest I enter?"

The two girls thought for a minute. "Your crow!"

Katie joined the excitement. "Yeah! You've been working on that bird for years. It's the best experiment you've got!"

"Okay you two, we'll see what happens. Now let's get some sleep. We've got a busy summer ahead of us."

That summer, Sarah got a rest from class work and used the time to hire contractors to start work on the mansion. She even contacted a well known Italian architect, Marcello Marvollo, to draw up the blueprints for the mansion based upon their requirements.

Katie and Zammie used their summers to prepare their curriculums for their first year as teachers. They did not see Sarah much that summer. Sarah spent her time at construction offices and on the phone while Katie and Zammie spent their time with other teachers and professors of the university.

By the time the summer was over, the foundation to the mansion had been laid and construction of the bomb-shelter-like basement had begun. Dexter helped to get all the legal matters over the building of the mansion out of the way in his spare time. Katie and Zammie were also prepared for their classes to begin.

With preparation over, Katie and Zammie's availability switched with Sarah's availability. The two Plier sisters now had the spare time to oversee the construction of the mansion while Sarah's time was put right back into classes and homework, not to mention an upcoming contest of fantastic proportions.

Frequent field trips to the construction site brought added excitement to the classes and kept the two girls involved with the construction during the day. When they weren't grading papers or writing tests and quizzes, the two girls watched the construction work, making sure everything on track.

Shortly after the start of the semester, when the construction crew approached the start of the support structure, Marcello Marvollo decided to pay the site a personal visit. Sarah pushed aside her work to be onsite for the occasion.

Marvollo stood no higher than Sarah's shoulders. The lines on his face spoke of age while Sarah determined that if his head still retained hair that some of it would be white by now. After studying his large, professionally made blueprints, he began walking around the site. His quiet but gruff voice sounded almost comical.

"Place main support here and here." Marvollo walked around the foyer area and pointed at various points on the ground. "Secondary support here and here and here." He pointed at various points around where he had pointed out the main support areas.

Sarah tried to talk to Mr. Marvollo about other matters, but she fell short of success. The only thing he wanted to talk about was the construction. Even that was not talk; it was more like ordering the construction crew in their next task. Still, Sarah could barely suppress her laughter at the comical mannerisms of Mr. Marvollo.

Although Marvollo's knowledge was never in question, construction was not a part of Sarah's studies. She wished she could have spent more time with him before he flew back to his home in Italy.

Chapter 6

The end of the first semester came too quickly. Sarah barely had any time to work on her animatronics crow for the contest. The second semester didn't offer much time either. She bought and installed some safe upgrades to the crow's hardware and completed the software she had written to control the bird.

Two weeks after the end of the second semester, Sarah, Katie, Zammie, and Sarah's mother travelled to the windy city of Chicago. They entered Soldier Field wearing name badges with a large number twenty-two. This number identified the display table set up for her experiment. It also placed Sarah in the order in which the experiments were to be judged.

One hundred tables were lined up around the edge of the field with a large stage set up in the center. Crowds already packed the stands to watch the contest unfold. Many of them wore suits and were undoubtedly there to be the first to purchase stock in the winning product.

"I'm a little hungry," Sarah said when they walked up to the table with the number twenty-two printed on it.

"We'll find some food. You get everything set up here." Katie and Zammie left Sarah and her mother to get everything set up.

"Sarah," her mother stopped and said to her as they pulled the computer equipment from their luggage, "no matter what happens, I want you to know that I am so proud of you. I remember when I gave you your first engineering and chemistry sets. You were so smart!"

"Aw, Mom."

"When those judges get here, you are going to show them what years of hard work has produced, hard work that you enjoyed so much." A tear began to form in Abby's eye. "I cheered you on at every success."

Sarah spotted Katie and Zammie on their way back with bags of food. "Okay, Mom, they are on their way back. We can talk about this later."

Abby quickly wiped the tears away before the two girls got close enough to see them.

The four of them were finishing up lunch when they saw the judges approach the first table. A lump rose up in Sarah's throat as she anticipated their approach to her table.

The noise of the crowd in the stands fell silent as Sarah shook the hands of Christopher and Robert, the two judges who walked up to her two hours later. "It's good to meet you, Sarah Mitchell. Let's see what you have here."

Sarah started the software and began sending commands to the crow. They were simple commands, telling the bird to walk around, bob its head, and make small noises. She then had the crow fly up in the air and circle the table. She then had the bird examine the table and land in its center. The bird landed perfectly in the center as directed.

"Hmm." Robert asked to take over the controls. Sarah let him.

He went through the same controls as Sarah did, only he had the bird fly a little further away from the table before having it land. The girls were not surprised when the bird landed perfectly for the judge just like it had done for Sarah.

The two judges thanked them and left for the next table. They left no clues behind to indicate their feelings on Sarah's bird. This annoyed them greatly. Sarah saw them judge experiments from small projects submitted to test the waters to space-age-like technology that was definitely years in the making. Sarah felt like one of the contestants who were there to test the waters. Unlike the first few tables, which seemed to take the judges a long time, they didn't spend very long at the remaining tables. Soon the judges were taking their places on the stage.

"Ladies and gentlemen! Welcome to this year's annual Scientific America Product Contest! Our grand prize winner will have his product mass produced and sold by Scientific America itself. Three other winners will receive a very generous monetary reward as well as an article in Scientific America about their product.

"It's been a tough contest thus far. We have quite a crowd of bright men and women who have brought extraordinary experiments! It was very tough to decide winners. To those who do not win, we have provided a lifetime membership to Scientific America.

"The first winner this evening, taking home the third place trophy and five-hundred thousand dollars, is an entertaining young man by the name of Jones, Joe Jones! His windshield monitor, while not yet ready for mass production, was quite distracting to say the least!" A dark-skinned man in his thirties walked to the center of the field and claimed his gold and silver trophy of the number three. Once he had made it back to his table, the judge continued.

"The second winner will take home the second place trophy and seven-hundred and fifty thousand dollars! This experiment, while brilliant and insightful, lacks the quality for this magazine to produce. Her breath analyzer will be a medical breakthrough, I'm sure! Melanie Griffin, please come forward and claim your prize!"

A young girl, fresh out of high school, with pig-tails and many freckles, ran to the stage. Her cheers were heard around the whole stadium. She grabbed her trophy and ran back to her table.

"Our first place winner has shown a great deal of talent! Her experiment will be in Scientific America one day, but unfortunately not today. She will have to settle with the first place trophy and a very generous prize of 1 million dollars! Sarah Mitchell, your animatronics crow will have to wait until another day for mass production. Please come and accept your prize!"

Sarah was overjoyed! She ran to the stage and accepted her prize with thanks. When she got back to her table, her mom and two friends greeted her with much cheering, hugging, and pats on the back. They calmed down and turned to see the award of the grand prize.

"And now we come to the long awaited time. The announcement of the Grand Prize Winner! This year's promotional product is one that is worthy of Scientific America! Thomas Jackson has broken past the limits of modern power consumption to produce a radio controlled car powered by solar energy! Everyone attending this event will receive a discount for the purchase of one of these amazing devices!"

An elderly man with a cane hobbled to the stage and received a sealed and notarized contract for the production of his experiment. The contract also entitled him to royalties from the sales of his product for the rest of his life.

Sarah left the event thankful that her friends had insisted that she participate. The new funds not only ensured the completion of the mansion but also allowed them to fully stock the place with food, furniture, decorations, and all other things they could think of.

Sarah spent that summer allocating the funds with the help of Dexter. Katie and Zammie spent their summer preparing for their second year of teaching.

The upcoming months seemed like an eternity for Sarah. Never had she been pressured with so much work. The only time Katie and Zammie saw Sarah now was for supper. But even then, she ate quickly and disappeared again.

The girls were glad when May came around. Not only did the time end the grueling undergraduate studies of Sarah, but it also brought a close to the highly anticipated completion of the mansion the girls were having built.

Katie and Zammie opened the two large, heavy doors revealing the grand foyer beyond. Dark finished cherry wood and majestic red carpet covered everything including a winding staircase that lead to both the second and third floor.

After touring the kitchen and labs on the first floor, the girls headed straight for their own master bedroom and their own bed. Neither of the girls took the time to look around their bedrooms but quickly changed and fell fast asleep.

Chapter 7

  The next morning, Sarah woke up in her new, four poster bed. She pulled back the heavy, dark purple curtains and blinked at the sun filled room. The first thing her eyes came to rest on was a large mirror set on top of a huge oak dresser. Sarah was thankful it had been already filled with her clothes. Her large walk in closet made it easy to find just the right outfit for the day.

  Sarah did not get dressed then, nor did she leave her bedroom. She decided that a long bath in her marble and crystal bathroom was in order. Steam filled the room as the scent of Champaign rose up from the bubbles around her.

  "And to think this only happens in the movies!" Sarah laughed as she made herself comfortable under the bubbles. Minutes later, she heard the sound of bath water running coming from the adjacent rooms. "Good; I'm not the only one up."

  Sarah took her time. It wasn't until the water started getting cold that she drained the tub and got out.

She put on a blue tee shirt she had picked up from a local zoo and some jeans before venturing down to the kitchen on the first floor.

She couldn't believe how large the kitchen was. Long counters with cupboards and multiple sinks and appliances lined the outside of the kitchen while a counter top island stood in the middle. She opened the massive steel refrigerator. "Wow! A fully loaded fridge!" She grabbed a jug of strawberry orange juice and set it on the counter beside the fridge. She then opened the freezer side of the fridge and cheered. "Waffles! Cherry and strawberry! I'm having both!" She pulled a cherry waffle and a strawberry waffle from their respective boxes and put them in one of three white toasters that sat only feet away from the fridge.

Minutes later, Sarah had the waffles buttered and covered with syrup and sat at the kitchen table, a large, oak table covered with a white table cloth, waiting for the other girls to arrive downstairs. She didn't have to wait long.

"She's eating chocolate!"

"No, she's eating cherry!"

"I know her better than you. She likes chocolate more than cherry!"

"That's not true. She eats chocolate covered cherries all the time!"

Katie and Zammie came flying into the kitchen, each one shoving the other one to the side, trying to be the first to the refrigerator. Katie got to the fridge first and flung open the freezer door. After quick examination, Katie dropped her head. "You were right, Zammie, she's eating cherry."

"Well, I want cherry too!" Zammie tried to squeeze by Katie with no luck. Katie grabbed two chocolate waffles and backed away from the fridge to let Zammie grab her cherry waffles. After toasting their waffles, the two girls joined Sarah at the table.

"So, what do you think, Sarah?"

"I like it! I hear we all took nice long baths." All three girls still had wet hair.

"Yes, we did! It was wonderful!"

They all leaned back in their seats at the same time. "This is the life."

Seconds later, they heard the sound of a helicopter in the distance.

Katie jumped up from her seat. "Come on, let's go to the roof."

Zammie jumped up too. "Yeah, come on, Sarah, let's go to the roof."

Sarah laughed. "You two are nuts! You go ahead."

"Come on, Sarah, you gotta come with us! You haven't even been on the roof yet."

"Is there even a way to get up there?"

"Of course there is, you silly! Now get up and come with us!"

"Alright, I'll go."

Sarah thought it would be silly to go up to the roof just to see a helicopter off in the distance, but she went with the two girls anyway. She began to get suspicious as she climbed the foyer staircase to the third floor. The sound of the helicopter grew louder.

"Now what are you girls up to?"

"Just follow us, you'll see."

The two girls led Sarah to the end of the hall on the third floor and up the flight of stairs to the fourth floor. At the end of that hallway, Katie placed her palm on a darkened square of the wall. A larger section of the wall nearby pulled inward and slid to the side revealing a small enclosure with a ladder. Zammie walked in and began to climb the ladder. She unlocked a hatch and beckoned them to follow.

Sarah ascended the ladder after the two girls and found herself standing on the roof of the mansion next to a helicopter pad. Sitting on the pad was a completely black helicopter. A short, heavyset man got out and ran towards them.

"Hello, Katie. Hello Zammie. And I'm guessing this is Sarah." He held out his hand to Sarah. "I'm Chopper, a friend of these two fine young ladies."

Sarah took his hand and shook it. "Yes, I'm Sarah. I didn't even know we had a helicopter pad on the roof."

"It appears the idea was Katie's."

"Would you like to have some breakfast? We have plenty."

"No, I need to be getting back. I only have this copter out for another thirty minutes. But I wanted to let you know that if you ever need anything, just give me a call."

"Thank you! We'll do that!" Sarah yelled as Chopper ran back to the helicopter.

The three girls spent the summer exploring the mansion and entertaining themselves with the games on the fourth floor. But as soon as the summer came to a close, Sarah disappeared.

Sarah started her first year of graduate studies. She spent all of her time in the university's library, her labs, the computer room in the basement, or her classes. The only time Katie and Zammie saw her was on rare occasions at supper.

This continued for five more years.

Sarah sat on pins and needles next to Katie and Zammie at the graduation ceremonies. Like every year, the undergraduate degrees went first. There were many with honors and double majors. Then came the graduate degrees. The students were called out in alphabetical order by their last name, so Sarah knew full well her place in the line. She waited, counting off each name as it was announced. When they reached Molly Mistician, Sarah froze; her name was next. But something happened that Sarah wasn't expecting. The next name announced was Mathew Mouseweaver. Then Misty Mutt was called. Sarah's eyes began to water. Was there a mistake in the list, and were they going to just forget about her? Was there something wrong with one of her grades that would prevent her from graduating? Sarah didn't want to answer any of the frantic questions bubbling up in her mind.

Then the university's vice president stepped up to the platform like he did every year for closing remarks. He looked down at Sarah and smiled. "It's been a privilege this year to have so many fine students graduate, not only from the undergraduate program, but also from the graduate level. There is one graduate who has not been mentioned yet. I have chosen to single her out because of her achievement. This individual has gone far above and beyond what has been required of her and achieved a level of knowledge that few will ever see or even know about in their lifetime. Sarah Mitchell is a picture of excellence and achievement! Sarah, would you join me here on the stage?"

Nervously, Sarah made her way onto the platform.

"Sarah Mitchell surprised us all by graduating with a double major eight years ago only to follow that with a third major. She comes back this year to amaze us all with a triple graduate degree."

Sarah had indeed completed three graduate degrees over the past six years, concurrently, spending two years on each one. She held off graduation ceremonies until all three had been completed.

"And her contributions to the Computer Science, Engineering, and Chemistry departments have been astounding! As a result of her contributions and on behalf of the president of this university, I would like to present her this honorary doctorate." He held up a degree certificate encased in a solid black frame. He handed it to Sarah and shook her hand. "It is now appropriate and respectful to refer to her as Dr. Sarah Mitchell." The auditorium erupted in clapping and cheering.

The ceremony ended, and Sarah stood outside greeting fellow students with her mother, two best friends, and Dexter. "Let's all go get something to eat," her mother announced to the group, "I have some things to talk to you about."

"Okay," answered Sarah.

"Sounds great!" replied Katie. Zammie nodded.

Dexter, though, shook his head. "I'm sorry, but I won't be able to make it. I've got a business meeting with some clients in half an hour."

"That's ok," said Abby. "Thank you, though, for coming to the ceremony."

"It was my pleasure." Dexter turned to Sarah. "Sarah," he paused. "You have accomplished something wonderful. Let's do something later, just the two of us." Sarah gave a nervous smile. "Okay."

Dexter said his goodbyes and left.

"Oooh, I think someone's got an admirer," commented Katie, giggling.

"He is quite a gentleman," added Sarah's mother.

Sarah started to blush. "Come on, guys, stop it!"

The group laughed as they headed to the mansion to get ready to go out to eat.

Chapter 8

Sarah drove her car into the parking lot of a new restaurant that she had never been before. The place was a huge, single story, restaurant. It looked like a large log cabin with its frame made up of large wooden logs. A large sign read "A Bear's Delight".

"Wow! Something new!" commented Katie as they all met in front of the entrance.

"I think you girls will like it," replied Abby.

When they walked inside, they were greeted with stuffed bears of all sizes and kinds. From large grizzly bears with huge honey pots to cute little mountain bears with small bee hives, the sight amazed the three young ladies.

They got a table for four and began looking over the menu. When the waitress came to get their drink order, Abby spoke up for them all. "We will all have water. We will also take the Bee Hive appetizer."

"Very good," replied the waitress. "I'll give you some time to look over the menus and be out with that appetizer right away."

"Wow, what a place!" Zammie scanned her menu with puzzled looks. "What should we order?"

"Well, on your first visit, I insist you all order a special. There is a surprise with each meal that will make the experience more memorable." Abby spoke with confidence. The girls all agreed.

"What's a Bee Hive?" asked Sarah.

"Well, it's a white sugar wafer in the shape of a bee hive. They cut it into sections. Each section is a honeycomb full of the sweetest honey you've ever tasted!"

"Wow! I can't wait to try it!" All the girls agreed with Sarah.

When the waitress came back with the bee hive and their waters, they were ready to order.

"I'll take the Traditional Bear with the Salmon," said Sarah.

"Ah, a popular favorite. What two sides would you like?"

"Hush puppies and apples."

"Good choice." She turned to Abby. "And for you, Ma'am?"

"I'll take the Premium Bear with the Black Bass. Cole slaw and a baked potato will do for my sides."

"Good choice. Perfect season for Black Bass." She turned to Zammie. "And what can I get for you?"

"I'm going to go with the Traditional Bear and Salmon. I'd like hush puppies and cole slaw as my sides."

"Good choice. And what about you, Miss?" She addressed Katie.

"I want the Exotic Bear! I'd really like to try the Rainbow Trout. And give me fries and cole slaw as the sides."

"Okay. I'll get this in." She took the menus and walked away.

The girls began to take sections of the bee hive and eat them. "This is great!" commented Katie.

"Yes, thank you, Miss Mitchell."

"No problem, girls. Just wait till you see your main meal."

Approximately ten minutes later, the bee hive was gone, and the waitress was bringing their main entrees. To each one's surprise, a stuffed bear was included with their order.

The waitress handed Sarah her plate and then handed her a traditional looking, light tan teddy bear with a stuffed salmon in one paw and a small pot of honey in the other paw. She also handed Sarah a small pot of dipping honey to go with her meal.

The waitress then handed Abby her plate with a stuffed, dark brown grizzly bear cub. The cub held a stuffed black bass in one paw and a small pot of honey in the other. Abby also received a small pot of dipping honey.

Zammie was handed the same meal and teddy bear that she had given to Sarah. Katie's bear stood out from the rest, though. She was handed a white, polar bear cub with a stuffed rainbow trout in one paw and a small pot of honey in the other paw.

All of the girls missed the waitress asking if they needed anything else except for Abby. She shook her head and said, "No, we are fine." Abby laughed as she watched the girls play with their stuffed bears. "Okay, girls, your food is getting cold."

Then, just like little school girls, they realized that their food had come *with* their stuffed friends. They looked down with surprise, grabbed their utensils and began to eat. It must have been good because their plates were completely emptied in minutes.

"Thank you, Miss Mitchell, that was great!" said Zammie.

"Yes, thank you!"

"Thank you, Mom."

"You're welcome, girls!" She flagged down their waitress. "Excuse me, Ma'am. We're going to need some coffee here."

"Okay. Any cream or sugar?"

"Yes. Just bring enough for everyone."

The waitress nodded and left.

"Wow, Mom, what's up?"

"Sarah, I've brought you here to talk to you about something. And I wanted you two here as well."

Zammie grabbed her bear and began to hold it tightly. She then gave the Sarah and Katie a scared look, prompting them to grab their bears so that Zammie wouldn't feel left out.

"I need to tell you about your father," Abby continued.

"My father?"

"Yes. I've been waiting for the right time to tell you."

"Okay. If you're ready, Mom, I'd like to hear about him."

Abby gathered herself while their waitress poured them their coffee.

"You're father's name was Doctor Kyle Smith. He was the best physician I had ever met. I was his first appointment when he started his practice in the village, the village where you were born. He was so nervous being fresh out of medical school with a fiancée on his heels. After many checkups, we knew we were spending too much time together. He had to make a choice, and so he did and chose the girl from medical school."

"Did you ever see him again?"

"Yes. We continued to see each other, although it was less frequent. Then I suddenly became pregnant."

"Me?" Sarah asked.

"Yes. I was excited and worried. I wasn't ready to care for a little child. At least I thought I wasn't. But I wasn't the only one who was pregnant. Dr. Smith's wife was also going to give birth to a little one. In fact, it happened on the same night that you were born.

"You were born first. You were so precious. How could I even imagine not being ready to take care of *you*? Dr. Smith let me hold you for a while before taking you to the nursery for some quick cleanup and measurements.

"Then Mrs. Smith went into her final stage of labor. I could hear them in the room next to mine. It went fast, but something was wrong. The baby wasn't crying. Then I heard a loud cry from Mrs. Smith and then silence.

"A few minutes later, Dr. Smith came sobbing into my room. 'She didn't make it.'

"I asked if he meant Mrs. Smith. He shook his head. His wife was fine, she had just passed out. His little girl was still born. He paced the room, sobbing, with his face buried in his hands.

"What I did next was not done out of love for him or dislike for you in any way. I still to this day do not understand why I did it, but I suddenly blurted out, 'Take my Sarah.' He stopped and looked at me, trying to understand what I had just said. 'You heard me, take my Sarah and give her to your wife. Tell her you were able to revive her. And make sure she has a good father; that's not something I would be able to give her on my own.' He left the room and did what I had asked."

"So, Mrs. Smith never knew?"

"Nope. She never had a clue. But then again, she never really got much of a chance to find out."

"Oh, why's that?"

"The next month, you attended your first and only Lottery."

"By the sound of your voice, that doesn't sound like a good thing."

A tear ran down Abby's cheek. "If only it were a good thing. Let me illustrate it like this. The name of the village you were born in was Wachmikilu."

"What? What kind of name is 'Watch Me Kill You'?" Sarah began to hold her bear a little tighter under the table.

"It's an appropriate name because of their barbaric annual ritual they call The Lottery."

"I know gambling is risky, but what could make it barbaric?"

"This event was not something the villagers looked forward to. It was an event where the winner and his entire family were stoned to death by the villagers."

"What!" cried Zammie as tears began to swell in her eyes.

"No way!" added Katie. "That's murder."

"How could they carry on with such an event?"

"I wish I knew. It was started long before I was born, and continues to this day for all I know."

"Did anyone ever try to stop it?"

"Only those who were about to be..." Abby broke into tears, shaking her head. "How could I have gone along with that horrible ritual for all my life? How could I have let them brainwash me into thinking it was okay? It almost cost you your life."

"What happened?"

Abby dried her eyes on a napkin and continued. "Your father drew the mark and was declared the winner, or should I say loser. The villagers chased down his entire family in the woods and killed them. Thankfully I found you unharmed. I was able to sneak you away to safety and fool the villagers into thinking that you had been dragged off by some wild animal."

Katie turned to Sarah. "And you thought gambling was bad...this is worse!"

"How did you, I mean we, get away?"

"The next morning, I had a sudden urge to leave the village. There was no way I could raise you and keep you hidden from the other villagers. I then realized that I just might be able to peacefully leave the village for good."

Abby explained that in order to leave the village for good, she must qualify to be the next mayor, who was above the requirement of the Lottery. This meant that Abby's parents and siblings must have been born, lived, and died as residents of the village and that she was the last of her family left in the village.

"I plead my case to the mayor, and he let me go. I left as fast as I could and never looked back."

They spent the next few minutes in silence, drinking their coffee and trying to digest the story Sarah's mother had just told them.

"Why didn't you tell me sooner?" asked Sarah. "You said Dad died of a heart attack and had his cremated ashes spread out over the sea."

"I know I should have told you sooner. I wanted to keep the truth from you until you were ready."

"I'm sorry, Mom, but I need some time to think this through." Sarah stood and turned to the girls, "See you back at the mansion." She then left, alone.

Katie found Sarah at the end of the hallway on the third floor of their mansion. She was staring into the starry sky. "Sarah, you ok?"

Sarah looked at her with a blank stare. Katie could see the trails on her face where the tears had streamed down her cheeks.

"The news is like an unclean set of stairs, it distracts you from where you are going." Zammie's smile disappeared as Katie and Sarah turned their blank stares to her. "Ok, neither funny or wise, I'll have to work on that. Sarah, are you ok?"

Sarah shook her head.

Five minutes passed before anything else was said.

"What are you going to do? More contests?"

Sarah suddenly leaped up and ran down the hallway.

"Now look what you just did!" commented Katie sharply. "Contests! Of all the things she needs right now, contests are not among them!"

But it was an upcoming contest that was indeed on Sarah's mind. The two girls found Sarah in her lab, examining her animatronics crow. "Ok, girl, time for an upgrade."

Sarah spent the next year putting her crow into as many contests as she could. She took each one as a personal challenge to improve the crow's software and mechanics. It helped take her mind off what her mother had told her about her father.

The following year, Sarah spent time caring for her mother as she battled with cancer. Shortly after Sarah's thirty-first birthday, her mother passed away. That night, Sarah sat in her room, staring out the window at the starry sky. She wondered just what had become of the village where she was born.

The next thing Sarah knew, she was down in her lab working again on her crow. She sat cross-legged on the floor surrounded by tissue, open boxes, and small tools.

"What are you doing?" Zammie stood in the doorway to the lab holding a pop-tart in one hand and a glass of milk in the other.

"Couldn't sleep either?" Zammie shook her head. "Well, I'm doing a final upgrade to my crow. She's got a mission to go on tonight."

"Oh, what's that?"

Sarah smiled. "She's going to see what's up in that village Mom told us about."

Zammie watched as Sarah turned on the crow. It walked around and bobbed its head. Sarah then picked up her computer and opened the program she had written to control the crow. She spoke out the commands as she typed them into the computer. The crow made a noise after each command acknowledging them.

"First, I need you to fly to these coordinates. Be on high alert the entire time. When you get there, find a hiding place, somewhere high, where you can see the meeting house. It's the large, single story building in the center of the village. If you detect any movement around the building, notify me immediately!"

The crow cawed twice, flew into the air, and circled the room. The crow then flew out an open window and disappeared into the night sky.

Sarah turned to Zammie who was still standing in the doorway. "Could you make a pop-tart for Katie and I along with some milk and meet us up in the dorm room?"

"Sure."

"Ok. I'm going to go get Katie; we'll wait for you."

Chapter 9

Sarah found Katie awake in her room. When they got to the dorm room on the third floor, Sarah hooked up her computer to the large wall monitor. They had the monitor installed in the wall so that they could watch whatever while sitting or lying down on the bunk beds.

It didn't take long for Zammie to join them. They all sat on the edges of their bunk beds eating their pop-tarts, sipping their milk, and starring at the night sky on the monitor as the crow flew towards its destination.

"How long do you think it will take for the crow to get to the village?" asked Zammie.

"Not more than a couple hours. She's great at getting somewhere quick."

Five hours later, the girls lay fast asleep on their bunk beds. An alarm went off! Sarah was the first up and turned it off. A large, old, one story building filled the monitor. There was a man walking around its parameter. Sarah maneuvered the crow to a broken window towards the back of the building. She peered inside, but there was no one there.

Katie and Zammie rubbed their eyes, trying to wake up and watch what was happening on the monitor. "Sarah, Zammie, I'm hungry. Would either of you like some breakfast while we wait?"

"I'd love some!" answered Zammie.

"That sounds like a great idea, Kate. We'll keep an eye on things here and let you know if anything happens."

"Okay. But I'm going to hold ya to it!"

Katie left the room.

"So, what do you think is going to happen?"

"I don't know, Zammie. It's the first Friday the thirteenth of the year and there are still people living in the village. My guess is that they will hold that annual ritual of theirs again."

"Do you think that same mayor will be there?"

"If he's still alive, I wouldn't doubt we'd see him there. He's got to be so old now."

The conversation went from clothing styles to cosmetics to hair styles before Katie came back with eggs, bacon, toast and juice for breakfast.

"Did I miss anything?"

"Nope. But you did miss Zammie plan her next outfit for her dinner party on Saturday."

"I did? Well that stinks."

The girls laughed.

As they ate, they watched one or two people enter and leave the building. Each one carried something out while others tidied up the place. When an old man with a cane entered the building, they began to take notice. He wore a scowl proudly on his face and many scars of time under a mat of grey hair. The girls knew that this had to be the mayor. He sat two bundles of cloth on the podium. The bundles were about the size of a baseball.

After a few minutes, a family of six entered the building and gathered on the right hand side of the mayor. They wore old clothes that looked a little shabby. Then a larger family of more than twenty entered the building and gathered on the mayor's left hand side. They wore much nicer and much cleaner clothes.

Once the initial commotion died down, the mayor spoke out in a loud, gruff voice. "Welcome to this year's holding of the Lottery. I trust you all know the rules. As I can see, this appears to be the final time we hold this event. Let's not waste any time."

Dogleg Pete tossed one of the bundles to a man on his right and tossed the other bundle to a man on his left. George Botmfeedhr didn't hesitate. To the surprise of the rest of his family, he opened a blank cloth. He laughed. "Finally! It took the last run of this event for us to finally come out on top!"

Christopher Thuderdyke opened his cloth to reveal a black spot. He didn't move a muscle. He just stared at George.

"I'm sorry, Chris, but it looks like you and your Thuderdyke clan will be doing the running now." Chris didn't move. After a minute, Chris and the rest of his family picked up their sacks of stones. "Chris, what are you doing?" The Thuderdyke family had formed a wall around the Botmfeedhr family. "Mayor, this is against the rules!"

Pete walked over and put a hand on George's shoulder. "Rules are rules, George. But I think in his case, you appear to be out numbered."

The mayor stepped outside the wall as each member of the Thuderdyke family pulled a large stone from their sack. In an eerie and pre-calculated maneuver, the Thuderdykes threw their stones.

The Botmfeedhr family didn't have a chance. They fell in seconds to the assault by the Thuderdyke clan. When it was over, Dogleg addressed the group. "Okay. Ladies, let's get everything ready to go. Men, let's take care of the bodies."

The ladies left the building, and the men dragged the bodies out behind the meeting house to a large, freshly dug grave. They threw the bodies into the grave and covered them up.

Then, over the next few hours, the remaining villagers loaded up a few semi-trucks and smaller vehicles with personal belongings and left the village.

Sarah instructed the bird to return home and turned off the monitor.

The three of them just sat there, thinking about how the village had been alive with people and now was going to be as empty as the blank monitor they stared at.

"Horrible," commented Katie.

"Barbaric," replied Zammie.

"And they think they can just get away with that?"

Sarah shook her head. "I don't understand how, but it looks that way."

"Sarah, what are you going to do?"

"I don't know. They are planning something. Somehow, I'm going to find out what that is and be there to watch it all crumble around them."

There was nothing more to say. The girls slowly got into their beds and got some much needed sleep.

The next morning, Katie and Zammie had made up their minds. Until the Thuderdyke plan was revealed, they wanted to keep busy. The best way they found to do that was to enter graduate studies of their own. Their new found goal was to become professors at the university.

Sarah still had her text books from her own graduate studies. She let Katie borrow the engineering books and let Zammie borrow the chemistry books. Frequent participation in scientific competitions kept the girls on their toes and at their best for their classes.

Sarah spent so much of her time supporting the girls that she failed to set aside enough time to compete in the contests herself. This gave Katie and Zammie prime opportunities to gain first place.

The next five years passed with ease. The girls sat at their favorite restaurant with Sarah on the night of their graduation. Sarah and Zammie decided to be daring and get the polar bear and rainbow trout. Katie stepped out and got something new, a brown bear and lobster.

"Congratulations, you two!" Sarah raised her glass in a toast.

"And big thanks to you, Sarah!" Katie raised her glass followed by Zammie. "We got the two positions that the Thuderdykes were after!"

Sarah had spent so much time helping Katie and Zammie obtain their graduate degrees that she didn't have much of a chance to figure out what the Thuderdyke clan was planning. "Girls, now that you both have graduated, there's something I need to do."

"What's that?"

"Well, Zammie, I've been wanting to visit the village."

"Are you sure? That was quite a dangerous place."

"I'm not sure anyone will even be there. As you heard the mayor, that was the final run of the Lottery. Just to walk through the village and see what would have been my home is something that I must do."

"Okay," replied Katie. "We'll come too."

Sarah shook her head. "Not this time, girls. I need to go alone."

"When are you thinking that you will leave?"

"Sometime next month. I think it would be good to go there around the anniversary of the day Mom took me away from there."

"Good. Now, let's think on happier things like..." Katie paused and winked at Zammie. Zammie winked back and both girls said in unison, "Happy Birthday, Sarah!" They both pulled wrapped presents from under the table.

"Now where did you get those?"

"Our car. Zammie out went and got them when you went to the restroom. Go ahead and open Zammie's first. She found something she knew would be perfect for you and almost spilled the beans and spoiled the surprise!"

Sarah took the small package wrapped in pink foil with a bright purple bow and opened it. Her eyes began to water when she saw the best friends' charm that had been split into three parts and placed onto gold necklaces.

When put together, the charm read, "Best Friends Forever." Sarah took the middle part and gave the other two to Katie and Zammie.

"That is perfect, Zammie. Thank you!"

The other two girls took their necklaces and put them on, as did Sarah.

"Now open Katie's present," added Zammie. "She looked for a long time to find this one."

Sarah took the present that was wrapped in the same paper as Zammie's present, only Katie's present had a yellow bow. "Cute," she commented as she opened the present and spotted a pink, stuffed pig standing in the box.

The girls laughed. "We thought you'd say that. Look under the pig."

Sarah lifted up the pig and saw a DVD case. She pulled it out and examined it. On first glance, it was thicker than a regular DVD case. The title read "Pastors' Wives Teach America."

"Wow! Thank you, Katie!"

"I know how much you like to hear what pastor's wives have to say. I heard about this collection from Mrs. Johnson. She has a session on there, by the way. Anyways, getting back to what I was saying, the collection was in high demand. Every place I went to was sold out or back ordered. I started calling around and found a place about two hours away. They agreed to hold their last copy for me, so there you go."

"I don't know what to say."

"There's nothing more to say. Let's get some dessert and go home."

The girls all got a dessert to go and travelled home in their separate vehicles. Sarah drove a needle nose

Porsche, and the Plier sisters drove a Hummer. It's just what they liked.

The days passed and speculations about what Sarah would find at the village abounded. At no point did Sarah waver on her decision to visit the village, although the Plier sisters did try to talk her out of it.

Finally, the day came for Sarah to leave. She hugged Katie and Zammie. "We'll be praying for you, Sarah," they told her.

Dexter slipped a small hand gun into Sarah's glove compartment, slid a thin, locked, metal box under the passenger seat, and handed the keys to the box to Sarah. "This is for your protection just in case something goes wrong."

"Thank you, Dex."

"Are you sure there's nothing more we can do to convince you not to go?"

Sarah shook her head. "Whatever it is, it's not going to work. But if anything does happen, I've got the best friends in the world to call on."

"And don't forget about someone else." Zammie pointed upwards. "Never forget that He's always with you."

"Thank you, Zammie."

Sarah got into her small sports car and drove off. Even though it was small, there was enough room to put just what she needed for the next two or three days.

The old Route 99 was not too far away from the university. Sarah made the turn onto the onramp and started heading north. The drive took Sarah over mountains, through valleys, across long spans of desert, and even over a lake before she caught site of the ancient forest that marked the end of the freeway.

It was evening when she passed through the tree line. The sun was just beginning to set. Shadows passed eerily by. A chill danced up Sarah's spine, and for the first time, Sarah began to question whether her trip was a good idea.

There was no sign and no warning. Sarah suddenly found herself amidst small, wooden houses. She recognized the construction from the video that her bird had brought back. She even saw the tire tracks left behind from the trucks used to carry the last remaining family away.

Then, before she finished comprehending the meaning of the tire tracks, a building approached her from ahead like an oncoming train. It was the large, one story building Sarah recognized to be the meeting house. Sarah froze. She felt like making a sharp turn to avoid a collision, when she realized that it was she who was approaching the building. She slowed her vehicle and parked it outside the front door.

When Sarah got out, she glanced around at her surroundings. There was still enough light for her to make out a main street that ran around the meeting house as well as the various small shops and businesses that had kept the town functioning.

Sarah couldn't help smiling. The town's appearance at that spot made her feel like she had just come home. She shivered, grabbed a bag, and walked inside the building.

A nauseating feeling struck without warning. Sarah saw the chairs shoved towards the sides of the large room creating a huge gab in the center. Trails of red went from one side of the gap to a side door. No one had ever cleaned them up.

Although she hated the feeling, it was perfect for what she was there to do. She sat down in one of the chairs, pulled out her laptop computer, and began to type.

Four hours passed. Everything was pitch black. There were no nocturnal creatures out that night. If there were any, they made no noise. Sarah rubbed her eyes. Time seemed to stand still.

Suddenly, the building filled with light! Streams of bright light flooded in from the windows almost blinding Sarah. By the time her eyes had adjusted to the light, a man came limping through the front doors towards her.

He looked as old as time itself. Sarah could see metal plates through tares in his clothing, although they looked more like coverings than protrusions. His face, a web of scars, repulsed her. A twisted, wooden cane supported his every movement. Sarah knew this could only be one man.

"Didn't expect to find anyone here." The whispery gruff voice floated through the room bouncing off the various dusty objects. He held out a gloved hand to Sarah. "Peter Snotgrasse. Everyone calls me Dogleg. I am the mayor of this village, or at least I was."

Sarah shook his hand. "My name is Dr. Sarah Mitchell."

Recognition and remembrance instantly appeared on Pete's face. "You wouldn't happen to be related to Abby Mitchell, would you?"

Sarah's mind struggled to comprehend the memory of the mayor and the danger it presented. She had no choice but to answer, but she did so with caution. "Abby was my mother."

"I thought you looked familiar; there's no mistaking that hair." Dogleg began pacing back and forth in front of her. "It's been thirty-seven years since Abby left this village. If you don't mind me asking, how old are you?"

"Thirty-five." Sarah answered quickly. She did not want to reveal her true age in fear that he might become suspicious.

"Wow. She must have found him before she left here. He must have been the reason why she left."

Sarah nodded. *If only he knew.*

Dogleg thought for a minute then moved on. "You said you were a doctor. What subject?"

Sarah told Pete about her accelerated education, her three majors, and her three graduate degrees.

Upon hearing this, Pete stopped his pacing and looked straight at Sarah. "That's quite an accomplishment. What are you doing right now?"

"Research and contests mainly."

"How would you like to be part of something spectacular?"

Pete continued pacing.

Sarah didn't answer. She now felt the bold, yet dangerous nature of the mayor and the reason why her mother wanted so much to get away.

"A rich family and I have come back to this village to tear it down and build an adventure themed tower in its place, but this place is not going to be like any tower you have ever seen before."

"So, what do you need *me* for?"

"I need someone with your brains to come up with a special power cable. This cable needs to be able to stabilize an erratic power stream without the assistance of a stabilizing device." Pete let Sarah think about it for a minute or two before posing his question. "Do you think it can be done?"

She nodded. "It's possible, with the right resources."

"Whatever you need. All equipment, materials and living expenses will be provided for you by us during any and all development and maintenance of the project plus extra for any commitments you might have elsewhere." He paused for a few more minutes to let the magnitude sink in. "Dr. Mitchell, we have been planning for this project since before you were born. I assure you, this project is no joke."

Sarah did not like the idea of working with Pete any more than she liked the idea of living in the village. She knew deep down that if she could just get them to trust her, she could probably setup something to backfire and finally bring justice to this murdering family once and for all.

"I will have to think about it before I can give you an answer."

"Not a problem. Let's get you some accommodations for the night. I know you don't want to sleep in here, and your car doesn't appear to be big enough to sleep comfortably in." Pete smiled as he glanced over and saw a lady approaching them. She had shoulder length brown hair, wire rimmed glasses, and a slender figure. "Ah, Charleen, just the person I need. Sarah, this is Charleen, our cook. Her trailer has an extra bedroom. I'm sure she wouldn't mind you staying there for a night or two."

"Naw, I don't mind at all." Her sweet and tender voice was flavored by a deep southern accent. "Come on, let's get your stuff and get ya settled in. Is that yer car out front?" Sarah nodded. "Mighty nice car fer these parts!"

They started to leave when Dogleg called after them. "Charleen, show Dr. Mitchell our web site. I'm sure she'd like to see the kind of resources that we have access to. It will help her decision."

"No problem, Boss!"

They exited the building and Sarah could not believe the sight. The village had just been flooded with a sea of vehicles of all sizes. There were passenger vehicles carrying family members, semi-trucks carrying supplies, and flat bed trailers carrying construction vehicles.

"Wow! Just how big is this family?"

"We're gettin' so big now that you can't hardly count us," replied Charleen.

"You're part of this family too?"

"Yup."

They walked east of the meeting house for a few minutes before coming to a clearing. There were dozens of recreational vehicles lined up in rows. Sarah saw large cables being positioned near the center of the group to provide power.

"This is where you are going to live?"

"For now. But it's only until the hotels get built."

"Hotels?"

"Yes. With the magnitude of the tower and the remoteness of the village, we are going to need somewhere nice for the visitors to stay. And we are going to need somewhere nice to live in ourselves. I'm not going back to staying in those old houses again."

Charleen led Sarah over to the largest of the RVs. "Mine is the largest," commented Charleen, "it has a portable kitchen inside big enough to feed everyone!"

They walked inside and sure enough, there was an extra-large kitchen inside. Charleen showed Sarah to her room and sat her things down on the bed.

"What did Pete mean when he said that this project had been planned since before I was born?"

"Well, for one thing, us Thuderdykes have been around for centuries. Although I do not agree with everything that we do, I pretty much have to live with it.

"Did you know that it was we who put Dogleg in power as the mayor? The family needed someone they could trust to manipulate the Lottery."

"Excuse me? The Lottery?"

"Yes, the Lottery. A sickening gambling event where we would pass out small bundles of cloth to every family in the village. The one with the black spot was stoned, and I'm not just talking about the person holding the cloth but the entire family!"

"Didn't anyone ever get arrested for murder?"

"Nope. Folk too scared to report it. And besides, the family's got such an influence over the law that nothing would ever happen.

"In fact, five years ago, we held the last Lottery. It was Thuderdykes against the Botmfeedhrs. And to add humor to insult, Dogleg gave the Thuderdykes the black spot. But we had way more in attendance than they did, so we gave them a run for their money, only they didn't run."

"What happened to them?"

"Did you see the red trails in the meeting house?"

Sarah nodded. There was a pause. Sarah was about to tell Charleen all about her past when she changed the subject. "Are you hungry?"

Again she nodded. Sarah had not eaten since lunch.

Charleen led her from the bedroom into a larger room next to the kitchen. She motioned to a small desk with a computer on it. "Pete wanted me to show you this." She brought up a web site on the screen.

At the top, the page read, "Thuderdyke Family Industries," followed by numerous links below.

"If ya do decide to help us out, what ya see on that web site is the kind of resources you'll have available to ya. Now if you will excuse me, I'll make ya my favorite midnight snack."

Sarah stayed up the rest of the night browsing the Thuderdyke web site. She had no clue what it was that Charleen had made for her, only that it was good.

In the morning, Charleen found Sarah with her face in her arms on the desk. A large order consisting of various voltage equipment and a variety of cables was displayed on the computer screen. A pad scribbled with calculations and percentages sat slightly under one arm.

Charleen put in the Thuderdyke payment code and turned off the computer. She then helped Sarah into her bedroom and into the bed. "Sleep well, Sarah," she whispered, "ya going to need it."

Chapter 10

When Sarah finally awoke, it was the afternoon of the following day. She wasn't going to do anything without a bath, so she took a long one. Afterwards, she ate some leftover lunch before venturing outside.

When Sarah exited the trailer, she noticed something odd. The homes and buildings of the village had all been torn down, all that is except for the meeting house in the center. Three very large plots of land around the meeting house had been dug up and concrete foundations were being laid.

She stood by the front door and pulled out her cell phone. It was time to give her best friends a call. After two rings, Zammie picked up the phone; they were at home.

"Sarah! Hold on, I'll get Katie." Sarah heard her call through the house. "Katie, Sarah's on the phone! Hurry up!"

Sarah knew Zammie had put her on speaker because she heard Katie come into the room a minute later.

"Sarah, we've been worried sick when we didn't hear from you. Are you ok?"

"I'm fine. The mayor and his Thuderdyke clan have returned."

"Sarah, I have a bad feeling about this. I'd get out of there if I were you."

"Are they going to start up the Lottery again?"

"No, Zammie, they aren't going to start that again. In fact, they are here redoing the entire village. They've torn down just about everything and are going to build a multi-million dollar tower of sorts. They've even asked me to research a special kind of power cable for them."

"And you agreed?"

"I haven't said yes, but I have started planning the research they will need." She walked to where she couldn't be overheard. "I need them to trust me, let me into their confidence, so I can look for a way to undermine what they are planning, throw a wrench into the system and make it back fire when they least expect it."

"You be careful," commented Zammie.

"Where are you staying? I hope they haven't put you in one of those broken down shacks."

"I'm staying with a very nice lady in a large RV. She's the cook for the clan. She dislikes what the others are doing, but she's afraid to say or do anything."

"Have you told her your story?"

"Not yet."

"Watch yourself, Sarah. I don't want to see you get caught up in all their problems."

"I will, Katie. How are your new classes going?"

"Brats, they're all little brats!"

"You know that's not true, Katie. Sarah, Katie is just frustrated because most of her students are Thuderdyke wannabes."

Sarah laughed. "Don't worry about it. I'm sure you can whip them into shape."

"Thanks, Sarah."

"Hey, Sarah, we've been down in the lab working on something super..." There was a thud and then silence.

"Sorry, Zammie, I didn't catch all that. What were you saying?"

"Ah, um," Zammie paused. "We're just working on some cool things for the kids. I thought..."

"Awesome, Zammie! Don't worry, I do like the idea. You must show me when I get back."

"Well, Sarah, we need to be going. We've got some stuff to get done before tomorrow."

"Ok. You two have fun, and try not to be too hard on those kids."

"Alright. You be careful, now. Let us know if anything changes."

They said their goodbyes, and Sarah walked back inside to find Charleen preparing her kitchen for supper. "Hello, Sarah. Want to give me a hand?"

"Sure, although I'm not much of a cook."

"Aw, don't worry 'bout that. Just follow my instructions, and you'll be fine. How's it looking out there?"

Sarah stepped into the kitchen and began rolling some dough for a large amount of biscuits. "Well, they've torn down almost everything. They left the meeting house standing. There are now holes dug for some large buildings, and they are pouring the foundations as we speak."

"Those will be for the three hotels. I've heard they are going to be skyscrapers! Everyone is going to be mighty hungry this evening. Let's make sure we make enough."

Sarah nodded, but her expression gave the appearance that she had no clue how she was going to manage that.

"Don't worry, Sarah. Just follow my lead, and everything will turn out right."

The meal turned out better than expected. Sarah found that she liked cooking.

"You know, I had fun today," Sarah told Charleen while they were cleaning up.

"I thought ya might. Wanna help me again?"

"Sure." There was a short pause before Sarah continued. "You know, it looks like I'm going to be sticking around here for a while. Would it be ok if I picked up some things from home tomorrow?"

"I don't see why not."

"Then that's what I'm going to do."

The next day, Sarah woke up early and drove half the day to get back to her mansion near Eagle Point University. She was glad to find no one there. Katie and Zammie were most likely in the university's cafeteria eating lunch. She took the next two hours and packed whatever she thought she would need and loaded everything into the truck that Charleen had let her borrow for the trip. Sarah then left a note for Katie and Zammie telling them that she had come back to get her stuff and not to worry when they found items of hers missing. She made it back to the village late that evening and went straight to bed. Katie and Zammie attempted to leave a message for Sarah on her phone sounding like they were upset with Sarah for not stopping in to see them. By the end of the message, they were laughing, ruining the joke.

For the next week, Sarah helped Charleen with the meals. When the meals were cooked, they were served under a large tent set up next to the RVs. Sarah was helping Charleen carry dirty dishes back to her RV when she spotted a brand new, white RV driving towards them. It was not quite the size of Charleen's RV, but it was larger than most of the other RVs. Sarah wondered whose it was.

She walked inside and sat down her load of dishes into the kitchen sink. The new RV pulled up next to Charleen's RV and a man with small glasses, a brown suit, and a clipboard like those mail men use got out of the RV and walked up to the open door and peered in. "Excuse me; I'm looking for a Dr. Sarah Mitchell."

"I'm Sarah Mitchell. How may I help you?"

"Yes. I'm here to give you your new lab."

"My new lab.?"

"Yes. Bought and paid for by Thuderdyke Family Industries. Your equipment and supplies are in the back. Now if you could just sign here." He pointed to the bottom area of his pad.

Sarah signed the pad, and he handed her the keys. As he turned to leave, Charleen came walking up. Sarah couldn't contain herself. She jumped up and down with glee, pointing to the new RV. "Charleen! They just brought me my very own RV!"

Charleen's smile widened. "I know the feeling. I felt the same way when I got my RV. Now let's go check it out."

Sarah and Charleen ran to the shiny white RV. Sarah threw open the door, being careful not to let it bang against the side, and stepped inside. It was like no vehicle she had ever been in before. On her left, just behind the passenger seat, there stood a large, voltage station. A kitchen sink and stove stood between that and a refrigerator.

Charleen sat down on the fluffy couch against the opposite wall from the door. "This is very nice!"

Sarah let Charleen relax while she ran to the back of the RV. "There's a huge bedroom and a bathroom like yours with a nice bath!"

"And it's all yers, Sweetie!"

Sarah came back from the other end of the vehicle with a large smile on her face.

Charleen glanced down at a long, rectangular box on the floor. "That must be yer cables that ya ordered."

Sarah thought for a second then snapped into realization. "Yes, you're right. I need to get those tested." She opened the box and began checking its contents. The package contained five different types of cable each with its own unique blend of metal composition. Of each type of cable, Sarah had ordered five different sizes. This brought the total number of cables in the box to twenty-five.

"Why so many cables?"

"Well, I ordered the different types to give me a good starting point and direction on what combinations of metal work best towards my goal. I ordered the different sizes to see if the diameter of the cable really matters with what I am trying to have them do."

"And what was that agin? I'm a tryin' to remember."

"Pete had asked me to make a cable that will stabilize a power signal without the aid of some pass through device. I'm pretty sure it can be done, I just need to find the right combination of metals."

"Ok. Sounds like ya know what yer doin'. I'll let you get to work. Don't worry bout the dishes, I'll get some of the boys to help me out."

"Thanks, Charleen."

"Don't mention it." She began to walk out of the door. Turning around in the doorway, she added, "And if ya need any help figurin' out this contraption, just give me a holla."

"I'll do that."

Sarah walked over to the voltage equipment and began to look it over. The gray machine stretched almost to the ceiling. The machine had a screen at eye level, some buttons and switches below that, two golden clamps on sliders, and a long slot towards the bottom about the size of a piece of paper.

There was a piece of paper on the flat surface between the clamps. Sarah picked it up and began to read it.

> Thuderdyke Electronics is proud to present, the new, customized O'Scope 9000! This O'Scope 9000 has been customized specifically for your needs. The nineteen inch display screen is now

industry standard. The buttons below the screen are, from right to left, a power button, a start and stop testing button, and a print button. A full keyboard has been installed for optimal input. To the left and right of the keyboard are two around knobs. Use the left knob to control the amount of amps that are pulled through the test conductor. Use the right knob to control the fluctuation level of the signal. Two clamps are provided on sliders to allow for varied lengths of conductors. There is also a printer located towards the bottom of the unit. The open slot is where the paper comes out, not where paper goes in. Use the flip up panel below the slot for access to the paper tray. You will also notice a barcode scanner hanging on the right side of the unit. Every test conductor purchased from Thuderdyke Electronics will come with a barcode. When scanned, the unit will be loaded with the exact specifications of the conductor for more precise test reports. Thuderdyke Electronics is a division of Thuderdyke Family Industries. The O'Scope products should only be serviced by a trained Thuderdyke Electronics technician.

Sarah laughed at the note and set it on the nearby countertop. She then pulled out one of the medium cables and attached either end to each clamp. She started the machine, and it hummed to life. After scanning the barcode on the cable, the screen displayed the exact makeup of the cable including the standard and maximum amperage that the cable could withstand.

Sarah adjusted the amperage knob and started the test. At zero fluctuation, the outflow was steady. Sarah slowly turned the knob to one. It was no surprise to her when the outflow remained steady. As the knob approached two, the outflow began to flutter. By the time the knob reached three, the outflow was just as erratic as the inflow.

After stopping the test and saving the results, Sarah went through the same test with the different sizes of that cable makeup. She was relieved when the tests came out the same for each size.

The second cable did not even make it to one on the dial. When she tested the different sizes, the test all came back the same. The third cable came closer to the two on the dial than the first cable did. This caught her attention. It was something she made a note of for when she calculated her next batch of test cables.

The fourth and fifth cables caused more of a fluctuation in the outflow than was generated. Sarah made a note to compare the makeup of those cables to see what metal could have caused the increase in fluctuation. Then again, maybe it wasn't a single metal that caused the increase but a bad combination.

"Looks like this is not going to be as easy as we thought," Sarah said to the machine, "this could take a long time to figure out."

That evening, Charleen helped Sarah move her things from one RV to the other. She also instructed Sarah on how to operate her new RV. Sarah was too excited to sleep, so she went back to her research of the cables.

She printed out the results from the tests and began to study them. It took three days before the calculations for the next batch of cables came to Sarah. When the cables came one week later, her fears were realized. Again, two of the cables caused an increase in fluctuation, and each cable had an entirely different makeup than both of the first two cables. Only one of the cables in this batch made it above one on the fluctuation dial.

This time, Sarah took an entire week to figure the calculations. She wanted to make sure she didn't miss anything. The result loomed over her like a gray cloud. Two cables made it about halfway between one and two on the dial. Two cables didn't make it to one, while one caused a fluctuation increase.

Sarah was frustrated and discouraged. She walked outside her RV and saw that one of the three skyscraper hotels were near completion. The framework for the massive tower was quickly nearing completion as well. She knew she was running out of time. Dogleg Pete would get restless because the construction of the tower would stop pending the discovery of the power cable they needed. Sarah was relieved when her cell phone rang and the person on the other end was not the mayor.

"Sarah, are you ok?" Katie asked when she heard the tone of Sarah's voice. Sarah explained the situation to Katie.

"Katie, I'm running out of time here. My calculations keep leading me down the wrong way. I end up with cables that either will not handle the fluctuations in the current or cables that cause an increase in the fluctuations."

"We're coming up there."

"What?"

"We're coming up there. Zammie and I will drive up there in two days."

"But what about your classes?"

"The students in both of our classes are right on track for where they should be. Zammie and I will have no trouble finding substitutes. We are coming up there, and there is nothing you can say to stop us."

Sarah smiled. "Thank you, Katie."

"Don't mention it, Sarah. See you in two days."

Sarah went right over to Charleen's RV and told her the good news. Charleen told Sarah that the girls were welcome to stay in her spare bedroom for as long as they decided to stay.

The next two days passed slowly for Sarah. When she wasn't helping cook or cleanup, she was studying her notes and the results of the tests.

"And they just gave this to you?" asked Katie when she stepped into Sarah's RV.

"Yes." Sarah was glad they arrived quickly and in time for supper that evening. Sarah showed the two girls her testing equipment and the rest of her living space before taking them over to meet Charleen.

"Well hello there! Y'all must be the two girls that Sarah has been talkin' so highly 'bout. I'm Charleen."

"I'm Katie and this is Zammie. We heard Sarah was a little discouraged and decided to pay her a little visit and see if there was anything we could do to help."

"That's mighty sweet of ya. I sure do wish I had friends like that!"

"Well, you do now. Come on, Katie, let's give her a hand with this meal she's cooking."

The girls all laughed and helped with the making of that night's supper.

"The hotels appear to be coming along quite well," commented Sarah as they sat under the big tent eating. "When are they expected to be done?"

"Sometime next month, from what I hear," replied Charleen.

"Wow that was quick."

"Well, Zammie, everything was planned out before we all got here. And when ya got as much money as the Thuderdykes, sometimes speed is not at all a problem."

"Then they won't be using any of my cables on the hotels."

"Nope. Dogleg's using those on the tower alone. He's got something big planned for that tower that he hasn't even told me about."

"Do you know anything about the tower?"

"Yes, Katie, but not much. Pete's calling it the Mars Occurrence Tower. It's an adventure tower dedicated to a failed mission on Mars."

"A failed mission on Mars?" Sarah looked puzzled.

"Yeah. I'm guessin' it's some top secret government thing. But they got the permission to build it, and I'm not seein' anythin' wrong with the idea. In fact, I'm excited and curious about what they are going to put inside. Aren't you? Just a little?"

"Sure. But you must remember that this is stemming from the guy who agreed with and presided over the Lottery. I think we should be cautious."

"That's true. I'll tell ya what, I'll try to get Pete to tell me a little more about what's going on with the tower. You just focus on getting that cable figured out."

That evening, Sarah showed Katie her notes and results of the tests. Katie scanned them for a few minutes and then began to look over the testing machine. With Sarah's permission, Katie performed a few tests of her own. She then left with Zammie for the night.

The next morning, the girls were finishing up breakfast in Sarah's RV when there came a knock on the door. Sarah opened it to a man in a brown suit brandishing a clipboard. "I've got a package here for a Dr. Sarah Mitchell." Sarah identified herself and signed for the package. "Here ya go, Ma'am." The man handed Sarah a long, rectangular package.

"What's that?" asked Zammie.

"My next batch of cables. Care to watch me test them?"

"We'd love to!"

Sarah powered up the O'Scope 9000 and started testing the cables. One test amazed them. Cable number three of that batch made it all the way to two on the dial. Katie studied the makeup of the cable. "I see it!" she blurted out a few minutes later. "You need to lower the amount of silver, and increase the amount of platinum and titanium. If you add a small amount of mercury, I think you'll have the cable you are trying to make."

"Wow, Katie, I think you're right! What do you think, Zammie?"

Zammie was already thinking way ahead of the other two girls. She handed Sarah a piece of paper with the names of the metals written on it next to percentages. "Try this combination."

"Thank you, Zammie. I'll send this in right away."

Katie shook her head. "It took the Chemistry grad to figure that one out." The girls laughed.

"Sarah, how long does it take to get back a cable you order?"

"Usually one week, depending on what the combinations are. Sometimes it's more; other times it's less."

"Well, we can stay another three days, and then we have to get back. Let's hope it comes before then."

Sarah put in the order, and the girls waited. After three days and no package, Katie and Zammie headed home. Sarah had told them that she would call when the package got there.

The very next day, the package arrived. Sarah signed for it and opened it up, revealing a single cable. She powered up the test machine and clamped both sides of the cable to the machine. She then scanned the bar code and cautiously adjusted the amp knob. Sarah started the test and slowly turned the fluctuation knob.

The outflow remained steady at one. This did not change at two or three. Sarah began to get excited. When the outflow was steady at four, Sarah prepared to give Zammie a call. As the knob neared five, the outflow began to fluctuate. At five on the dial, the outflow was just the opposite of steady.

Sarah froze. Her best lead had just turned up nothing. She laid down on her couch and fell fast asleep, exhausted.

Suddenly, Sarah awoke to the sound of an alarm. It came from her O'Scope 9000. The nearby faucet had broken, and water was streaming onto the cable causing the power fluctuations to jump way beyond what the machine was rated to handle. Sarah rushed to the sink and turned off the water. She then took some towels and began to dry off the machine. In her haste to dry everything off, she didn't take the cable off the clamps, but dried it while it was still attached.

After a few minutes, the alarm stopped. Once everything had been dried off, Sarah glanced over at the outflow monitor. It displayed a steady current. Sarah glanced down at the knob on the right; it was on five. Sarah quickly turned the knob to zero and began the test again. She slowly turned the knob all the way up to six, which was the maximum fluctuation that the machine could produce. The outflow remained steady.

Sarah looked at the time; it was midnight. She quickly picked up her phone and dialed the mayor's number.

"I've found it!" she yelled when she heard the mayor's voice.

"Found what," replied the gruff voice, "and who is this? This had better be important!"

"Pete, it's me, Sarah. I've found how to make a cable that will do what you need it to do!"

Dogleg Pete's mood suddenly changed. "Good job, Sarah, you've just earned yourself a bonus! Now I need you to order us a large amount. I need about one hundred miles of cable with a diameter of half an inch and another one hundred miles of cable with a diameter of one-eighth of an inch."

"I'll make that order right now."

"Tell them we need the cable ASAP! They can start off with one mile of each size. Make the second shipment five miles. The following shipments should be ten miles each until we reach our order. Make sure all of the cables are thickly shielded. Tell them we will make additional orders as needed. Once again, good job, Dr. Mitchell!"

The mayor hung up. Sarah rushed to her computer and made the order. She made sure she gave specific instructions on how to make the cable and about treating it with water. She even scanned the machine's results and sent that in along with her order.

She looked at the time again. It was twenty minutes after midnight. Sarah wondered if she should give the girls a call. She gave in and dialed the number.

A half asleep Zammie answered the phone. "Hello?"

"Zammie, your calculations worked! I had to treat the cable with a little water, but in the end, it worked!"

"Sarah! That's great news! I'll get Katie."

"No! Just go back to sleep. Tell Katie in the morning. I just wanted to let you know that it worked and thank you for knowing your stuff."

"Thanks, Sarah. You get some sleep too."

"I don't know if I can, but I'll try."

Sarah was able to get a couple hours of sleep. At breakfast, she told Charleen the good news.

"Looks like we chose the right gal for the job," Charleen told her. "Good work!"

Chapter 11

Six days passed. Dogleg called a meeting under the big tent. "Ladies and gentlemen! It is my great pleasure to announce that after only a short period of research, Dr. Sarah Mitchell has found a solution to our power problem! In six months from now, we will have our completed tower!

"We will hold a private showing three days before the grand opening for all of you plus friends and family. I would also like to announce that the main hotel is done and ready for business. The Illusion and Hallucination will be the smaller hotels with only twenty floors; they still have some work left, but I promise that they will be done by the time the tower opens. The Delusion is the main hotel with twenty-five floors where we will all live. Let's all pack up and move in. There is a covered and locked parking lot to the west of the Illusion where you can park your RVs. They will be safe there.

"I thank you for coming. Now let's get moving!"

Three days later, Sarah sat in Charleen's luxurious suite on the fourth floor relaxing in a comfortable couch looking at the construction of the tower. She had already unpacked everything in her own suite and needed the company. Charleen enjoyed the company since her job of cooking the meals for everyone had been taken over by the new hotel staff.

The structure of the tower had already been built. It looked like a huge square. The shiny black outer layer had already been started on the ground floor. The girls could tell that the building was looking to be a real marvel. No doubt they would be getting tourists from all over the globe.

Sarah and Charleen were both almost asleep when Charleen's phone rang. "Is Dr. Sarah Mitchell there?"

"Yes, she is. May I ask who is calling?"

"This is the front desk. We have a package waiting for her."

"All right. We'll be down to pick it up in a few minutes."

Charleen hung up the phone.

"A package? I'm not expecting a package."

"Well then, let's go see what it is."

The elevator ride down was filled with anticipation. When they got to the front desk, a large, brown box stood on a small cart.

"Looks like a wardrobe box if you ask me," said Charleen. "Let's get it back to your room."

The two girls thanked the desk clerk and wheeled the package up the elevator and into Sarah's room. There was a note attached. Sarah opened that first.

"It's from Katie and Zammie!" she exclaimed.

"That's nice. What does it say?"

"It says, dear Sarah. We are sorry we couldn't bring this with us before to give to you directly, but it wasn't done by the time we left here. Some professors and we have been working on this ever since you started working for Pete. It's a hazard suit and arm cannon." Sarah opened the box to get a look at what the girls were talking about in the letter. She pulled a golden helmet out of the box first. The visor on the helmet was green and shaped in a wide V. The next part of the suit was a black jumpsuit. Sarah slipped it on. Even though it fit perfectly, she determined that it wasn't supposed to be worn over her clothes. The next two items were pairs of boots and gloves. Each one had its own seal ring to secure it to the jumpsuit.

The last piece to come out of the box was the arm cannon. This marvel of technology was golden with slices of green glass, like the visor on the helmet, running down the sides of the barrel. Sarah put her arm into the cannon and felt that it was incredibly light weight and came up comfortably to her elbow. The letter talked about the cannon having an infinite power supply when worn with the whole suit.

"The cannon you now hold is a quad phase cannon, meaning that is has four types of discharge," continued the letter. "Each type of discharge can be accessed by rotating the barrel clockwise and is indicated by a certain colored glow on the barrel. The discharge type can also be changed using two buttons near the grip inside the unit. Yellow is the normal discharge. Be careful; it's powerful enough to blow a hole in a wall. The second type of discharge is red which stands for a super heated plasma discharge. Be careful what you aim this discharge at. The target will melt instantly. The third type of discharge is purple. This type is designed to create havoc in electronics. And last, but not least, the blue discharge. The blue discharge will freeze its target.

"We hope this new personal equipment will be of comfort to you. Please use it should their high tech gadgets get away from them. Also, feel free to take the included wall hanging for target practice. It has been tested to withstand all four types of discharge from the cannon.

"As always, you are in our prayers, Sarah. We hope you enjoy the suit!"

"Wanna try it?" asked Charleen.

A large grin formed on Sarah's face. "Yes. Let's give it a shot."

They laughed as Charleen took out the wall hanging, which was like a large bed sheet, and hung it on one of her living room walls. It covered almost the entire wall. "If you can hit the broad side of a barn, you should have no trouble hitting this!"

Sarah laughed as she closed the curtains of the wall size window that looked out the back of the hotel towards the tower. "I don't think I'll have a problem then." She disrobed down to her underwear and slipped into the suit. She had been right, it fit comfortably. She then put on the boots and turned the seal to lock them in place. Next she put on the gloves and locked them in place. When her right arm was all the way inside the cannon, it locked automatically onto her suit sleeve and glowed yellow through the green glass slices.

"Make sure ya know which button is the trigger," commented Charleen, "or try to find a safety switch. Don't want that thing to go off when ya don't want it to."

Sarah popped on the helmet with one hand.

"Wow! You look like a spacey bounty hunter of some kind!"

"Can you hear me?"

"Yes, but it sounds like you are talking through a walkie-talkie."

"Same here. Must be some sort of intercom built into the helmet. Now let's see what this cannon can do."

Sarah aimed the cannon at the wall and pulled the only button that was near her forefinger. A bright yellow gradient shot from one end of the cannon to the other end, underneath all of the glass slices, followed by a yellow bolt of energy bursting from the end of the barrel. It hurtled towards the wall and hit the white wall covering, burst into bright yellow sparkles, fell a few inches, and then disappeared. Sarah was knocked back a step or two by the recoil of the cannon.

"Wow! This thing's got quite a kick."

"Try it again!"

Sarah readied herself. This time, she thrust her arm forward slightly as she pulled the trigger. This helped dampen the recoil. The discharge leaped from the barrel like before and shattered into sparks before disappearing.

"That looks quite dangerous! There must be a safety switch somewhere."

Sarah began to feel around the grip that was inside the cannon with her thumb. She found a spot that felt different from the rest of the handle. After some pushing from the side, a small part of the grip moved, and Sarah felt a small button underneath. "Watch out, I've found a hidden button. Let's see what it does."

She aimed the cannon at the wall and pressed the button.

The lights on the cannon went dim and then began to pulse red. Sarah waited, but nothing else happened. She pulled the trigger. Again, nothing happened. Sarah pulled the trigger, nothing. It was as if the power had been turned off. "I think I've found the safety switch."

"Good."

Sarah pushed the hidden button again and closed the button's cover. The red pulse disappeared and the yellow glow came right back. "Watch out, Charleen, I'm going to try switching the discharge."

Charleen had walked up to where Sarah had been shooting the wall hanging. She quickly backed away as Sarah raised the cannon and rotated the barrel; the glow from beneath the green glass changed color. "That's interesting. If I turn it back…" Sarah rotated the barrel counterclockwise. The glow changed back to yellow. "I think I've found how to change the type of discharge."

After rotating the barrel again, the glow changed to red. Sarah braced herself, took aim, and fired. The intense, red ball of energy exploded just like the yellow bolt, causing red sparks to dance around the impact area.

"That's some hot stuff!"

The heat was evident yards away from the point on the wall where the impact took place.

"Let's see if I can do something about that."

Sarah rotated the barrel again, and the glow on the cannon turned blue. She fired, and a blue shard shot from the barrel. It burst into bright blue sparks and left a cool mist in the air. The heat had vanished.

"Awesome! Try the last type."

Sarah rotated the barrel, and the cannon glowed purple. The discharge was a dark purple ball surrounded by bright purple arcs that danced around rapidly.

"You've got quite a weapon there. What are you going to do with it?"

"I'm not sure yet."

Sarah found two buttons on the exterior of the cannon that were the same distance apart as her thumb and forefinger. When she pushed them at the same time, the cannon gave an unlocking sound and became loose. Sarah was then able to slide it off her arm. The glow slowly faded after the cannon had been removed. Sarah then took off the helmet and the rest of the suit before climbing back into her clothes. She stored the suit in the back part of her closet and left with Charleen for supper.

Chapter 12

Sarah told Katie and Zammie just how amazing the suit and cannon were and how thankful she was, even though she had no clue when or how they were going to be useful. She also told them about the upcoming grand opening and how it was less than six months away.

"You have to get Dexter to come as well. This is just the thing that he would enjoy."

"Wow, Sarah, that's exactly right! You're getting to know him pretty well. We'll let him know right away."

Sarah informed Pete that she would be bringing three of her closest friends to the grand opening of the tower. He told her that he would let the proper people know.

Over the next five months, Sarah watched, from the outside, as the tower came together. She also tested the cables as they came in before turning them over to the electricians.

"Sarah, I'm glad to see that you are safe," Dexter said to Sarah as they rode the elevator up to the seventh floor of the hotel. Katie and Zammie had run off to visit the other two hotels. As Sarah looked up at him, he pushed back her long, red hair. She turned to face the glass and looked out at the finished tower. Its massive, black shape almost blended in with the darkness. Blades of red light shot from the bottom of the five story structure to the top illuminating two towers that appeared to grow right out of the roof. The towers gave the tower an overall height of eleven stories.

Dexter placed his hands on the guard rail in front of them. "Looks like quite a building," he commented. "I've been told you've not been inside yet."

"That's right. I guess I'll just wait and see what the mayor has in there with the rest of the public."

"You mean to tell me you were never curious enough to go sneaking around?"

"Nope. I bet that place is full of secrets. I'm not sneaking around a place like that alone."

"Are you two getting off?"

Sarah turned to see a cleaning lady holding the doors to the elevator open. Sarah glanced at the carpet outside the doors and realized that it was the seventh floor and hurried off with Dexter behind her.

"Yes, thank you."

Sarah and Dexter turned the corner as the cleaning lady let the doors to the elevator close. She led Dexter to his suite, which was right across from hers. She bid him good night and entered her suite.

The next morning found everyone who had been invited to the grand opening standing outside the foreboding tower. Sarah and Charleen were of the few who had friends to invite. Most of the Thuderdyke clan had been chosen to work inside the tower except for a handful like Charleen. At best, the crowd for the grand opening was only one hundred people.

As the crowd stood shivering in the morning air, Dogleg Pete walked in front of four sets of double doors, all made completely out of a dark, smoky glass, with a microphone in his right hand. His voice boomed over the crowd.

"Welcome to the grand opening of an experience you will never forget! I give you, the Mars Occurrence Tower! Dedicated to that failed mission on Mars, this tower will stand as a testament to those who lost their lives in a great attempt to resurface the ancient Martian culture. We honor their memory and give you a chance to live their lives by journeying to their home on the Red Planet.

"Stay as long as you'd like; leave whenever you please; purchase a souvenir to take home; but most of all, enjoy your visit."

Pete pressed a button, and the doors opened. Sarah followed the crowd into a theater like entrance followed by Dexter, Katie, and Zammie. Attendants stood by five pods that looked like miniature space ships. They were beckoning people to climb aboard. Since these pods were the only things in the entrance other than the ticket booths, Sarah, Dexter, Katie, and Zammie all piled into the center pod. Sarah guessed that each pod could hold at least twenty people, and when using all five pods, one hundred people could easily fit in just one trip.

After buckling up, the doors to the pod closed and the pod began to shake. Screens all around the inside of the pod popped into life displaying the inside of a hanger.

"Welcome aboard the Aqua Pod, Thuderdyke Family Industries' premier launch pod," came a woman's voice from the pod's speaker system. "This pod will take you safely from Earth to the Phoenix III, the halfway point between Earth and Mars." The screens display the simulation of the pod lifting into the air and soaring out of the hanger and into the night sky. The pod pivoted and swayed to give the impression of movement.

"I don't believe it!" whispered Dexter into Sarah's ear, "it's all based on a video game!"

"What," she whispered back.

"It's all based on a video game. Sarah, have you ever heard of a manned mission to Mars, let alone a FAILED mission ON Mars?" Sarah shook her head. "Right. This tower is based on a fictional video game that I used to play when I was a teen. Once word gets out, everyone who used to play the game will flock here like crazy. Dogleg is sitting on a gold mine!"

Minutes later, the pod approached a large, round space station. It docked, and the movement stopped. Doors opened on the left and everyone exited the pod into a large room. Once everyone had exited their pod, all five pods were pulled back through heavy, black curtains and disappeared.

Sarah looked around. Two hallways led away from the room on either side while one hallway went straight ahead of them further into the station. The floors, walls, and ceiling had a gray metal look to them with pipes and cables exposed and running everywhere. Sarah saw a gift shop on the left side of the northern hallway and a small fast food restaurant, called the Earth Set Grill, on the right.

"My guess is that they'll head for the gift shop."

Sarah laughed as Dexter's prediction came true. As soon as the crowd thinned, Katie and Zammie made a bee line towards the gift shop. Sarah and Dexter chose the eastern hallway, which turned out to be a tunnel of sorts, to walk down first.

The tunnel simulated a ring that ran around the entire space station. On either side of the walk way ran a guardrail. Outside of the guardrails were curved windows stretching from floor to ceiling. The window on the right displayed the vast expanse of space while the window on the left displayed the gap between the ring and the space station. At various intervals, the tunnel came to a junction with a connecting tunnel into the station's core.

"This is quite a good representation of the Phoenix III," commented Dexter.

"So, what part of the game did this station represent?"

"Not much. The game starts with the player on his way to the station. The player can choose to stay on the station as long as he wants running errands for credits (money). He can then stock up on supplies like food and water using those credits.

"The player can also interact with the travelers to Mars. He can listen to their stories about how they heard of the Mars opportunity and hear about their anxiety to be a part of something truly marvelous. Or the player could interact with those coming back from Mars on their way to Earth. These travelers are filled with fear, full of horror stories from devilish experiments that are rumored to be taking place on Mars."

"Sounds like the player gets mixed feelings about going to Mars."

"Right, but every player ends up getting on the next launch pod that takes them to Mars."

They walked in silence before coming to the junction that was on the far side of the station. "Shall we venture in and see the station?" Dexter said in a comical tone.

"Yes, we shall," replied Sarah, laughing.

Sarah and Dexter proceeded down the connecting tunnel into the station. They passed by many rooms used by the player for staying the night on the station before venturing to Mars or to Earth. All were locked but one, but all had windows from which to view their interior.

"I've stayed in quite a few of these rooms in the game," remarked Dexter as they walked into the open room. "It's quite a treat to finally be able to walk inside one."

"You aren't planning to stay the night, are you?"

Dexter laughed. "I'm almost tempted to, but no." He went to pick up a computer pad that was sitting on the desk in the room when he discovered that is was bolted to the desk. Upon examination, everything was bolted to whatever it was sitting on. "Ingenious! They allow you to walk in, but you can't take anything out. I like it!"

They stayed in the little room for a few minutes before continuing down the corridor.

"I wonder what kind of power this station runs off," commented Sarah.

"That would be in the engineering section. That area was blocked off in the game. I'm sure it's blocked off here as well."

"What about those errands you mentioned? Do you think we could do one?"

Dexter thought about it for a minute. "I'm not sure, but I know of one errand that would be easy for them to do. Let's head to the south west of the center of the station."

Sarah followed Dexter to an intersection where people were gathering. Dexter spotted an elderly man dressed in a grayish brown suit and a brick red vest. Dexter pointed to the man. "There, that's old man Johnny. He should be asking people to find his dog." Sarah and Dexter approached the man, who appeared to be looking for something. "Excuse me, Sir, are you lost?"

"Why hello there, young whippersnapper! No, I'm not lost, but my dog is. Would you be so kind as to help me find him? I've got fifty credits for ya if ya do."

"Sure, we'll help you find your puppy," answered Sarah.

Johnny went back to his searching.

"So, where do we look first?"

"Follow me."

Sarah followed Dexter to the Earth Set Grill near the entrance. A small, black lab chased his tail near a trash can. "There's the puppy!" Sarah pointed towards trash can.

She approached the dog and tried to coax the dog to come to her. It didn't work. The dog ran behind the trash can instead. "How do we get him?"

"We need some food." Dexter walked up to the counter. "Do you have any dog food?"

The young man behind the counter dressed similarly to Johnny but with a yellow vest looked up at Dexter. "I've got this hot dog or a dog biscuit."

Dexter turned to Sarah. "This is one of the tricks of the errands. It's supposed to make you think. You see the dog is here because he smells the food. It's more likely that he smelled the hot dogs rather than the dog biscuit." He turned to the man behind the counter. "I'll take the hot dog."

He handed the hot dog to Dexter in a napkin. Dexter walked towards the trash can and held out the hot dog. The dog walked out from behind the trash can and began to bite the hot dog. The next second, the dog had vanished.

"What happened to the dog?"

"Hologram, I guess, and a pretty good one at that. Let's go back to Johnny." Dexter tossed the hot dog into a nearby trashcan.

When they got close to where Johnny was, the dog appeared out of nowhere and ran up to Johnny. Johnny petted him furiously before turning to Dexter and Sarah. "Thank you for finding Fido! Like I promised, here's fifty credits."

Johnny handed Dexter a large, gold coin. Dexter then gave the coin to Sarah. "Here you go. You can have this."

"Thanks." They stood there for a few minutes watching Johnny and his holographic dog. "Are you ready to go on to Mars?"

"Yes. Let's give the girls a call first and see where they are."

Dexter called Katie from his cell phone. "Katie, Sarah and I are going on to Mars. Where are you and Zammie?"

"We're on the west side of the station walking through the outer ring. You two go ahead. We'll be along shortly."

"All right. Hey, let's meet on Mars in about half an hour for some lunch."

"Sounds good to us. See ya then."

Sarah and Dexter walked to the center of the space station. The center was a large, round room with heavy, black curtains, like the ones at the entrance, in an oval around the center of the room. Seven pods stuck out of the curtains on all sides. They were smaller than the launch pods at the entrance.

People had gathered and formed lines in front of the pods. Each line contained around four or five people. "Five minutes!" came a woman's voice over an intercom overhead. "Five minutes till the pods leave for Mars. Please pick a line and wait patiently."

Sarah and Dexter picked a line with four people and waited. A couple minutes later, people dressed in outfits like the one Johnny wore, approached the line. Only one "Johnny" approached each line.

"I'm Gus. I'm on my way to Mars, what about you guys? They want me because I'm a scientist! They want me to study some artifacts they found on Mars. I can't wait!"

"Cool," replied one of the other people in line. "We are on our way to Mars too."

"Attention, pods are ready for boarding. Please stand clear until the pods have come to a safe and complete stop."

The pods slowly approached the lines. When they came to a stop, a door on the side swung open and a "Johnny" got out of each pod. Each one limped up to the line near his pod. "Beware the ghosts on Mars," Sarah heard him say. "Do not go to Mars. Terrible things are being done on Mars. I beg you, do not go." The "Johnny's" all ran off towards the direction the first "Johnny's" had come.

Sarah and Dexter boarded the pod with the rest in their line. The smaller pod appeared to seat around ten. After a minute or two, the door closed and various screens popped into life around them.

"Thuderdyke Family Industries welcomes you aboard the Cardinal VIII. This newest pod in the cardinal line of launch pods had been proven to cut travel time to Mars in half. The cardinal launch pods are smaller than the Aqua pods due to their need to withstand entry into the harsh Martian atmosphere." The pod began to lift and move. The screens showed the pod rising out of the center of the space station into open space. The next thing they knew was that they were on their way towards the red planet, Mars.

"Our destination on Mars will be in the center of the Mars base camp. This site is the building blocks for Mars City, a huge complex designed to bring life back to Mars. When you get to Mars, be sure to stop by the general store and purchase any access cards you feel you might need during your stay. The food court will provide you with only the best Martian cuisine! And for those of you who are brave at heart, visit the Marine Headquarters for some firsthand combat training.

"For now, just sit back and enjoy the ride. We will be landing shortly."

One minute after the woman had stopped talking, the pod began to descend through the Mars atmosphere. They descended through the center of a massive, dark complex before coming to a stop.

The doors opened and everyone got out onto a web of cat walks. The lighting was very poor. Sarah leaned over the side of the guard rail and stared into the blackness below. The lack of light gave the appearance of standing over a bottomless hole in the ground. After everyone had exited their pod, the pods moved silently through the heavy, black curtains.

"No way!" Dexter blurted out suddenly.

"What?" replied Sarah.

Sarah turned and saw Dexter run over to a lighted display case. Inside the case Sarah saw a dark metal gun. An open box of shells sat on its side by the gun with shells spilling out around the inside of the case. "What have you found, Dex?"

"It's a combat issue shotgun! Only the best weapon of any shooter game!"

"Good eye," commented a man whom Dexter had not seen. He was wearing the same type of outfit that Johnny wore. He stood holding a gun that looked exactly like the one in the display case. Beside him sat a large box containing dozens of guns. The man turned toward the crowd in the distance and began speaking in a loud voice. "Snot blasting shotguns! Get your snot blasting shotguns right here! Blast Beelzebub's beasties! Decapitate the

Devil's demons! Maul Martian monsters! All with your very own snot blasting shotgun!"

"How much for one?"

"Only one hundred dollars, Sir."

"That's not bad. Must be special replicas! Good thing I've been having some good cases lately. I'll take two." Dexter handed the man two one-hundred dollar bills. The man took them and handed him two shotguns from the box. "Here you go, Sarah." Dexter handed one of the shotguns to Sarah, who had been studying the one in the display case. She took the gun with gratitude, but at the same time not knowing what she was supposed to do with the thing.

"Excuse me, Dr. Sarah Mitchell?" asked the man selling the guns.

"Yes?"

"It's nice to actually get the chance to meet you. We wouldn't have had this tower ready by now if it hadn't been for you."

"What do you mean?"

"As you probably know, we've been planning something like this for years. Before we came back to the village, the mayor was pulling his hair out trying to find a way to safely power his big experiment. After none of us could find a solution, we came here anyway, hoping a solution would present itself in time. That's when you showed up."

"Well, I'm glad I could be of help."

"You two be careful. There are strange stories going around about this place."

Dexter thanked the man and began to look over the shotgun he had just purchased. Engraved in a small silver plaque on the side was the name N.E.V.E.S – Nuclear Experimental Virtual Exterminating System. Dexter pointed the shotgun at the floor and pulled the trigger. A click sounded from the middle of the gun. He pulled the trigger again, and again the click was heard.

"You have to pump the shotgun first."

As he pulled back the pump under the barrel, an authentic sounding shotgun cock came from the gun. Sarah pointed to the chamber above the trigger. "What was that?"

Dexter pumped the shotgun again and saw an empty shell casing fly from the right side of the chamber and disappear. At the same time, a full shell appeared out of nowhere and loaded itself inside the chamber from the left side. "Awesome!" replied Dexter.

When he pulled the trigger again, the shotgun gave off a loud bang, and a simulation of pelts burst from the end of the barrel before vanishing.

"What's this for?" asked Dexter as he pointed to a small readout on the top of the shotgun. It displayed a small zero.

"That's your point counter," replied the man selling the guns. "If you should run across any dangerous creatures here on Mars, the gun will tally up points as you defend yourself and those you are with."

Dexter thanked the man again and headed towards a nearby door. Sarah followed. They were glad the guns came with shoulder straps.

They passed through the heavy metal door as it slid open automatically, revealing a large square room. A long, dark corridor stretched out in front of them as well as to their right and to their left. Above each doorway, a sign hung with bright wording. The sign to the right read, "Food, Supplies, and Administration." The sign straight ahead read, "Lodging, Recreation, and Marine HQ." The sign to the left read, "Utilities."

"Which way?" asked Sarah.

"To the right. I almost always go to the right when coming to a junction in a video game."

Sarah and Dexter followed the corridor until they found themselves inside the Mars Supply/Gift shop. Postcards, trinkets, souvenirs, and Mars T-shirts where intermingled with combat gear, fake ammo, and security access cards of all kinds.

Dexter caught sight of the access cards and approached the counter. "If they continue to do this tower like the game, I'm thinking that we are going to need some access cards."

The man behind the counter noticed Dexter's interest in the cards and spotted Sarah. "Dr. Mitchell, welcome to the Mars Supply Center."

"Thank you."

"You wouldn't happen to have your Thuderdyke staff card on you, would you?"

"Yes, I have it right here." She pulled the card, which was hung as a pendant around her neck, from underneath her shirt.

"That card will grant you access to all of the visitor areas granted by these cards plus your special staff access. Is this guy with you?" He pointed to Dexter.

"Yes. This is Dexter. He's a friend from the university."

"I can see you are familiar with our tower. I tell ya what, in thanks for what you have done, Sarah, in helping us get this tower up and running, I'll give your friend five access cards for free."

"Thank you." She turned to Dexter. "Go ahead and pick out the cards you want."

Dexter did so while Sarah called Katie and Zammie.

"Ok. We'll be there in fifteen minutes."

Once Dexter was done picking out the cards he liked best, he and Sarah walked through the rest of the store and into the Mars restaurant, the Red Planet Rotation. Since Mars' calendar year was twice as long as Earth's, the restaurant owners decided to rotate the cuisine every two days.

The restaurant was a waited restaurant. Sarah and Dexter were taken to a seat and given menus. Although they ordered drinks, they waited for Katie and Zammie to arrive before ordering any food.

It didn't take long for the girls to find them; there were only a handful of people in the restaurant. The majority of the visitors were exploring the tower.

"This place is awesome!" commented Katie as she set her shotgun underneath the table. There was a bright pink sticker with her name on it stuck to the stock. Zammie had done the same thing to her gun with a green sticker. The girls were going to battle for points, so they didn't want to get their guns mixed up.

"So, what are you two going to do next?" Dexter asked the girls after they ordered.

"We're going to check out the recreational facilities before finding some monsters to maul," answered Zammie. "What about the two of you?"

"I'm a little curious about the utility area," replied Sarah.

Dexter smiled. "I think that would be a good place for us to check out."

During the meal, everyone talked about how much the tower looked like the game, but no one said anything to Sarah about anything that was to happen next. When they were all finished, they walked back to the main junction. Katie and Zammie each pumped their shotguns and headed through the eastern path towards the Marine HQ while Sarah and Dexter headed through the path towards the utility area.

"Get your gun ready," Dexter said to Sarah.

Sarah pulled the shotgun from her shoulder and pumped it. "Expecting trouble?"

"You could say that."

The lights were dim, and some were even blinking. Sarah almost didn't see it at first, but she realized what it was and took aim and fired. After a couple shots, it vanished. "Good shooting," commented Dexter. "Zombies are the first enemy in the game. They're not too tough to kill."

"So, what part of the game are we at right now? I saw you smile back there when I mentioned coming here first."

"All right, I'll tell ya. We actually skipped part of the game in coming this way. The game starts out with the player reporting to the Marine HQ first. That's where the girls went. Your first orders are to visit a very skeptical officer in the administration area. You find the officer monitoring a delicate experiment when things suddenly go wrong. The officer immediately tries to radio a fleet of ships that are on its way to Mars when the power goes out.

"It's the player's job to then report back to Marine HQ for further orders. Communications start coming in from all over the facilities that monsters are attacking out of nowhere. The player is then sent here, to the utility area, to restore power. It's good to get a jump on the girls once and a while."

"Do the girls know the game like you do?"

"Know it? I would say they have mastered it! They've gotten the better of me on almost every occasion!"

"Oh? How so?"

"The game has a multiplayer mode where players can go head to head with each other. The first time the girls ever challenged me, I should have known they had something up their sleeves. They teamed up against me and beat me every time they played me. Watch out!"

It was Dexter's turn to shoot up a zombie. One jumped out just in front of Sarah. "Thanks."

They continued to kill zombies one by one until they got to a large, circular room. A tall, round device stretching from floor to ceiling stood in the center of the room. "That's the power generator. We need to find a way to turn it back on."

As they walked into the room, dozens of zombies stepped from out of the shadows. Sarah and Dexter started firing as fast as they could. Two or three fell, but no pathway appeared to open to the generator through the crowd. They kept firing.

"This is exciting!" shouted Sarah, "but I don't see any way of getting through."

"You're right. It looks like we're a little outnumbered."

"Well that's what you get for getting ahead of the game." The voice came from behind them.

"Yeah! Say, K, do you think we should help them out?"

"I don't know, Z. What do you think?"

Zammie pointed her shotgun at the group of zombies that Sarah was firing at and started shooting.

"I guess that means we're helping."

Katie joined Dexter and began shooting at the group he was firing on.

Within minutes, the crowd had thinned and a pathway through the monsters opened up. Sarah ran through the opening, firing as she went.

Suddenly, the lights came on, the zombie's vanished, and a bright yellow glow began to circle the center of the large, round device in the center of the room.

"Good job, Sarah, you found the power switch!" shouted Dexter.

"Beginner's luck!"

"Try to catch up to us this time!"

Katie and Zammie rushed through a newly opened panel in the wall and disappeared up the ladder inside.

"What's up there?" asked Sarah.

"Level two."

Sarah followed Dexter up the ladder into a dark corridor. The corridor twisted and turned before ending at a wall of glass. Sarah looked through the glass into a large room with many tables, counters, and cupboards. About a dozen scientists dressed in white lab coats studied beakers of dirt, rocks, and odd looking artifacts using high tech equipment.

"Searching for Martian secrets?"

"No," replied Dexter, "they are looking at the simple stuff, everyday Martian culture. What they're studying gets sent back to Earth. We're not to the secret stuff yet."

As they stood there watching the scientists, Sarah gasped. A piece of the ceiling fell and an emaciated creature with dark red skin fell through the whole in the ceiling. The creature began jumping around the room before attacking the scientists. After a dramatic performance, the scientists each fell to the floor, and the creature jumped back into the ceiling. Then next thing Sarah and Dexter knew, the creature had fallen through the ceiling in front of them. They aimed and fired. After few shots, the creature exploded into nothing.

"Ok, what next?"

"Let me see. I don't think the girls know about your all access staff card. Let's use it to our advantage. This level is all about going from one end to another searching for various access cards. Follow me."

Sarah followed Dexter around some corners and down some corridors until they reached a large, metal door with an access panel next to it. The panel glowed red with the word "Locked" in the middle. "Use your card."

Sarah pulled out her card and slid it down the side of the panel. The panel changed to green, and the door opened.

Dexter ran through. "Hurry, get in." Sarah did so, and the door closed behind them. Sarah felt the floor rise. The room they had entered was an elevator.

"Level three already?"

"Yup. Wasn't that quick?"

"Sure was. I wonder how far behind the girls are."

"I'll give them about ten minutes until they are in here as well."

The elevator stopped, and the door opened. Again, Sarah followed Dexter out of the elevator and down a long corridor. Dexter readied his shotgun, and Sarah did the same. "Keep your eyes on the lookout. This is where it gets tough."

Just a few steps ahead, the corridor came to an intersection with another corridor. Straight ahead and to the left, the corridors where lit by blinking lights. To the right, the corridor plunged into complete darkness.

Suddenly a man came running up to them. The man grabbed Dexter's arm. "Stay away! Stay away!" He released Dexter's arm and went running into the darkness. Seconds later, they hear a yell and then silence. Then a bright red fireball came flying out of the black. Sarah and Dexter ducked.

They backed up as a charred human figure came lunging out of the dark corridor. He had another fireball in his right hand, ready to throw it at them. Sarah and Dexter took aim. It took them a few more shots than it did with the zombies before this creature dissolved into nothing.

"We're getting close," commented Dexter. "Let's hurry."

Sarah followed Dexter through corridor after corridor. Along the way, more fireball throwing creatures slipped from the darkness into their path. The points on their guns kept on getting higher with each creature.

They also passed by many locked doors. "I guess they aren't ready to open the secret experiments to the public yet," commented Dexter as they passed the third locked door.

They rounded another corner and saw something they didn't expect to see. Katie and Zammie stood mere feet away. They stood next to a part of the wall that was a slightly different color than the surrounding sections. They were looking through handfuls of access cards.

"I'm not finding it, Z, are you sure you don't have it?"

Zammie shook her head. "I'm sure we picked one up."

"How did you two get here so fast?"

Katie turned and faced her brother, shoving a handful of access cards in his face. "Did you think we would spend all that time trying to find these things! No!" She lowered the cards. "And now we can't seem to find the most important one."

Dexter held up a navy blue card from his pocket. "Oh, you mean this one?"

Katie looked up and snatched the card from his hand. "Yes. Thank you." She placed a hand on the wall behind them and it opened up, revealing an access panel. She slid the blue card down the side and a door opened. She and Zammie hurried inside. "Come on, hurry up! Get in!"

Sarah and Dexter walked through the door before it closed. It was another elevator, only this one began taking them higher than just one story.

"I think this is the elevator to the portal room, what do you think?"

"I think you're right, K," replied Zammie.

After a minute of listening to some video game like elevator music, the door opened. They walked out into a large room where a crowd of people crouched behind a barricade of debris shooting at monsters as they flooded out of a large stone oval filled with fire on the far side of the room.

"Has anyone tried shooting the portal?" Dexter called out.

"Yeah. It doesn't work," came back someone's reply.

Then all of a sudden, the lights came on, and the monsters vanished. The fire in the stone oval extinguished and there stood Dogleg Pete. He wore a tan, hands free microphone and when he spoke, his voice was amplified throughout the room by a large speaker array.

"Ladies and Gentlemen, welcome to the great experiment! I hope you all have enjoyed the adventure so far. I would now like to introduce you to the highlight of Martian technology." He pointed to the stone oval. "The Martian teleportation device." There erupted a sound of awe from the crowd.

"First things first, though. I need everyone to back away from the barricade." Everyone did as they were told. Then large hooks on heavy metal wire descended from the black ceiling. Staff took the hooks and attached them to various parts of the barricade. Once all of the staff had given their thumbs up, the barricade began to be lifted up until it disappeared into the ceiling. "Now if I could have everyone find a yellow line and stand on it. Only one person per line."

After everyone had found a line, parts of the floor slid away and theater like seats rose up in their place. Everyone then took a seat.

Pete began to pace back and forth in front of the device. "The teleportation device was discovered on Mars during a routine scouting mission. The scientists on the mission did not want to bring the device back to Earth for fear of what the device might do in a different atmosphere, but they knew that the device needed to be studied. So they used the cover up story of colonizing Mars as an excuse to bring back more teams to Mars to set up a base camp and eventually a fully functional Mars City.

"As you have been discovering through touring this tower, all did not go as planned. Teleportation was realized, but at the cost of many human lives. And now, Thuderdyke Family Industries has brought this marvelous piece of Martian technology to Earth for final testing purposes." He turned to the stage where a few staff members stood at computers stationed behind the device. "Boys, let's light this thing up!"

The device was positioned perpendicular to the audience. The people sitting on the right and left of the center saw a beautiful blue barrier appear in the center of the stone oval. The barrier had an appearance like the surface of water. Those who sat in the center of the audience had to ask the people next to them what they saw.

"But you are probably wondering, how can we have a proper test of a teleportation device without somewhere to teleport to? I have that answer."

Pete signaled to one of the staff members. The entire right wall of the room blinked, and the room was flooded with the afternoon sunlight. "You are all sitting in the top of the western tower. Across the way is the eastern tower." A large monitor on the left side of the room popped into life displaying a similar room with a crowd of people, a stone oval device, and a large monitor. "As you can see, there is a similar room, like this one, in that tower. Can you hear me over there?"

The crowd in the monitor waved. "Yes, we can hear you," came cries from the crowd through the speakers in the room.

"Good. Now, I am going to teleport myself to that room by simply walking through this device." Pete stepped up to the device from the left side and stepped through it. He did not come out the other side.

"Look!" someone in the crowd said and pointed out the side window. A bright blue ball of light shot through a large tube that ran from tower to tower. Seconds after the light disappeared on the other side, Pete appeared, on the monitor, stepping out of the stone device in the eastern tower.

"Can you hear me over there in the western tower?" His voice came over nicely through the speakers. The crowd replied back. "Yes, we can hear you."

The crowd in both towers erupted in clapping and cheering.

Pete quieted the crowds. "Well, you all can see me, let's prove it to those in the other tower, just in case they doubt." Pete walked over to the glass wall.

An elderly man got excited and shouted to the rest of the crowd, "I see him! I can see him! He's really over there!"

Both crowds erupted again in clapping and cheering.

Pete walked over to the stone device, this time from the right side, and stepped through, again, not coming out the other side. The blue light appeared once again in the connecting tube between the towers and shot back over to the western tower. Seconds later, Pete finished his step through the device.

"I bring you, Martian teleportation, the highlight of Martian technology! I hope this has all been fun for all of you. Be sure to return tomorrow where we will be offering a full day of fun, adventure, shooting, and this exciting demonstration! In just one week, we will be opening this tower to the rest of the public. Feel free to stay as long as you'd like."

Pete made a gesture with his hand, and large elevator doors opened in the back of the room in both towers. "To facilitate a quick exit, please use these elevators. There is one in each tower. They will take you right to the entrance.

"I ask that you leave the tower for the rest of the day. We need to get these rooms set back up for the stragglers who are waiting to see the show. I would not have you spoil the surprise for them.

"Again, I thank you all for coming and making it this far in the tower. Enjoy the rest of your stay."

Pete walked to the back of the stage and began talking to the staff. The small crowd made its way to the elevator. Sarah, Dexter, Katie, and Zammie did not make it inside the elevator due to lack of space. The doors closed. It took around five minutes for the elevator to return, at which time the group was able to fit inside with the remaining members of the crowd.

Sarah, Dexter, Katie, and Zammie left the tower and went back up to Katie and Zammie's hotel suite.

"Wow, that's quite a place!" said Katie.

"Yeah, I know!" replied Zammie. "It actually felt like we were walking through the game!"

"I agree. And those shotguns were a big help."

Katie patted her shotgun. "Yup, Z and I are going back tomorrow to shoot up some more monsters! What did you think about the place, Sarah?"

"Well, it's not like anywhere I've ever been to, that's for sure. What did you all think of that teleportation show?"

"It looked a little fake to me."

"Fake! Dex, that demonstration was awesome! How on Earth could you say that it was fake?" Katie looked cross at her brother.

"Well, for one thing, the teleportation took too long."

"But we saw him disappear and reappear in the other tower," replied Katie.

"I saw that, but he was the only one who was teleported. Think about that. And he didn't let anyone from the audience come up on the stage and examine the device."

"Maybe he was hiding his secrets, like magicians do, or maybe it's all real, like he says it is."

Dexter shook his head. "Even magicians let audience members come up and examine their devices. Helps put a sense of realism to their act. No, I think the

mayor is hiding something, and I don't think it's just
magician parlor tricks."

Chapter 13

Katie sighed. "Leave it to Dex to ruin a good act." She turned and faced the girls. "I don't know about you two, but I'm tired! Sarah, go get changed into something comfortable and meet us back here. Let's take a nap."

"And I guess I'm not invited," commented Dexter.

The girls all laughed. The laughter stopped when Katie said, "No."

"OUT!" continued Katie, sharply. She pointed to the door. "Don't make me pounce you like I used to when we were kids," she continued, giggling.

Dexter stood. "Then I bid you adieu." He turned and left the suite.

Twenty minutes later, Sarah, Katie, and Zammie snuggled cozily in their own make shift sleeping bags.

"I agree with you, Katie, that was a spectacular show!"

"Right, Sarah. And I'm not buying Mr. Fake's impression of the show either! I think it was real. Just look at how he stepped through the thing on one side and didn't come out the other. That's pretty hard to fake if you ask me."

"You've got a point there. It appears that Pete and the Thuderdykes have accomplished what they set out to do, even though I don't like their methods."

"Yeah, it would seem that way. Say, do you think you would ever go through that thing?"

"Nope." Sarah's answer was fast.

"Why not?"

"Because even though I helped him power that experiment, I've seen enough science fiction to know that I'm not about to have my body processed by some computer and sent through cables only to have another computer try to put me back together again."

"Hmm, a good point. Hey, Z, what would you do? Would you go through that thing?"

When Sarah and Katie didn't hear an answer right away, they turned and saw that Zammie had fallen fast asleep.

"I guess that's our cue."

Sarah and Katie decided not to say anything else. They too soon fell fast asleep.

The next morning found the four intrepid explorers entering the tower along with most of the visitors from the previous day. Katie and Zammie had challenged Sarah and Dexter to a point war. Just as they passed through the entrance, though, Dogleg Pete walked up to Sarah.

"Dr. Mitchell, I need to have a word with you."

"Ok," Sarah answered and turned to face Dexter. "I'll give you a ring on your cell when I'm done."

Pete led Sarah through a staff door and through the space station to its far side. There they passed through another staff door and into a room with many computers and computer stations.

"Sarah, I can't begin to thank you for what you have helped us accomplish here. Letting your mother go from the village thirty-seven years ago was probably one of the best decisions that I have ever made. But I need to ask for your help for just a bit longer.

"We have no one on staff that is as brilliant as you are. I need you to remain on staff here for three months and train my staff on how to best keep this place up and train them on your new cabling. At that time, you will be free to go back to Eagle Point or wherever you would like to go. You will also leave with a very handsome retirement check. What do you say?"

"Mayor Pete, that sounds like a very generous offer. If you will permit me, I would like to discuss it with my friends first and pray about it. Can I let you know in a day or so?"

"Fine. I will give you a few days. But first, as a token of our appreciation, please take this." Pete picked up a small package from a nearby desk and handed it to Sarah.

"What's this?"

"It's a complete, Mars Occurrence Tower staff uniform. I had Charleen get your measurements. Whether or not you stick around, it is yours as well as the RV; you've earned it. Follow me."

Pete led her out of the computer room and down the outer ring of the space station until they came to a junction on the far right back corner. Two large doors, like restaurant kitchen doors, stood in the side wall with small round windows towards the top. Pete unlocked the doors with his card, and they walked inside. It was a locker room.

"This is where you will keep your belongings that you need during work." Pete pointed to a side room. "You can change in there. Feel free to try on the uniform and wear it during your visits. While wearing it, you will have unrestricted access to the entire tower. All I ask is that you do not reveal any secrets that you get from the other staff to anyone. Can I have your word on that?"

Sarah shook Pete's hand. "You have my word."

"Then I will leave you to get changed. If any part of the uniform is not the right size, just get the alterations to Charleen; she will take care of it."

Pete left, and Sarah took the package into the changing room and opened it. Inside sat a solid black, button up dress shirt, a black pair of casual dress slacks, a pair of black, steel toes shoes, a pair of black socks, and a gold name plate. The shirt had a large, red, realistic looking lightning bolt on the back with dozens of forks and branches arcing away from the center line. There was a smaller version of the lightning bolt on the top right of the front of the shirt above the words "Mars Occurrence Tower". The gold name plate had the name "Dr. Sarah Mitchell" engraved in black letters with the title "Electrical Specialist" engraved below the name.

She tried on each piece. Each one fit perfectly. When she had put on the entire outfit, she called Dexter on his phone and told him to meet her at the space station's fast food joint. She also told him to have Katie and Zammie there as well. She then stuffed her clothes inside the package and made her way out of the locker room and over to the Earth Set Grill.

Sarah found a table that was big enough for all four of them.

"Ah, miss, waiting for friends?" asked a nearby waiter when he saw that she didn't stand at the counter to order.

"Yes."

"You wouldn't happen to be Dr. Sarah Mitchell, would you?"

"Yes, that is my name."

"Wow! Someone famous! I never thought I would get to meet someone famous! Listen, lunch is on the house. What would you like?"

Sarah smiled and silently laughed. "Well, now, I'm not sure. What would you recommend?"

"If you're expecting friends, I'd say go with the big value meal. Four rocket dogs, four planetary burgers, four saucer fries, and four moon drinks."

"Ok, I'll take that."

"Right. Now what would you like to drink?"

"Water. Give us all water." Sarah smiled. "That's what Mom would do."

"Good choice, Ma'am. Fresh, ice cold water from a mountain stream in Alaska is the only water Thuderdyke Family Industries serves its customers. I'll be right out with your order." The waiter walked away and disappeared behind the counter.

Sarah looked towards the entrance and saw Dexter walk in followed by Katie and Zammie. She stood and waved to them.

"Wow, Sarah you look....Sexy!"

"Katie!" Sarah snapped.

Katie laughed. "What do you think, Dex?"

Dexter smiled. "You look good in that outfit. It looks very handsome."

"Well, thank you, Dexter." Sarah smiled at him, and then glared at Katie.

They all took a seat at the table.

"So, does this mean that you have decided to join their staff?" asked Zammie.

"No," Sarah replied, shaking her head, "but it does seem like I already am a part of the staff. Pete has asked me to stay on for another three months."

"Why? What would you be doing?"

"Training his staff on how to keep this place up and running. He said that there was no one on his staff as qualified as I was."

"Are you going to do it?"

"I don't know, Dex. What would you do?"

Dexter pumped his shotgun. "I'd tell everyone to stand back!" They all laughed. "If it were up to me, I would probably stay. It's not every day I would get to work for a real live video game adventure. But that doesn't rule out who it is that is heading this project. And let's not forget that this video game he's basing this tower on was a doomed mission. Things may not turn out ok in the end."

"Don't listen to him, Sarah," added Katie. "He's just trying to scare ya! And besides, we've already seen the doomed part." She pumped her shotgun as well. "It's great shootin' up monsters, right Z?"

"Right, K!"

Just then, the waiter brought the food to the table. "Here you go. And I see your friends have arrived."

"Yes, they have. Thank you."

He sat down the food and drinks and then left.

"So, you see, Sarah, you have to stay. Come on, do it for us. Besides, Z and I want to come here for free whenever we want to." Katie and Zammie began to giggle.

"Alright, girls, I'll think about it. Now let's eat before it gets cold."

Sarah and Dexter grabbed a hamburger while Katie and Zammie grabbed a hot dog.

"Oh, Sarah, Z and I would like you to join us for some monster killin'. What do you say?"

"Yeah, come on Sarah, it will be fun!" chimed in Zammie with a mouth full of food. "We can call you S."

Sarah nodded. "Ok. What about Dex?"

Dexter shook his head. "Don't worry about me. You girls go and have fun. It looks like you may not see much of Sarah over the next few months. I'll be ok. I'll do some exploring on my own."

For the rest of lunch, Sarah and Dexter ate in silence while Katie and Zammie whispered strategy to each other. After they were done, Dexter headed towards the Marine HQ while the girls headed straight for level two.

By the time they got to the tower elevator, Katie and Zammie's scores were over a million while Sarah's score was barely half that much. The final firefight at the top of the tower brought Sarah's score close to a million and brought Katie and Zammie's scores over two million. The show was the same; only this time, it was conducted by a member of the tower staff and not by the mayor.

The following day, Sarah told Pete that she accepted the position for the next three months. Pete gave her a key to one of the lockers, and Sarah decided to store her suit and cannon inside it. She concealed the suit and cannon inside a large, duffel bag.

She also bid farewell to Katie, Zammie, and Dexter. They needed to get back to Eagle Point. Katie and Zammie had classes to teach and Dexter had a new case to begin. They all thanked her for inviting them out and told her to keep an eye out for Pete.

Half an hour after they left, Sarah threw her shotgun over her shoulder and headed out of her room. She didn't go to the tower, though; she went to Charleen's suite. "Who is it?" she called from inside.

"It's me, Sarah."

"Come on in, girl! I'm in the kitchen."

Sarah opened the door and walked in. She found Charleen in her kitchen, cooking. "Need any help? I might be able to remember a thing or two that you taught me."

"That's awfully sweet of you, but I'm almost done here. Why don't ya just set your things over in the livin' room. Supper's almost ready."

Sarah walked into the living room and set her shotgun on the large, pink, fluffy couch. "Heading to the tower?"

"I was thinking about it," replied Sarah as she came walking back into the kitchen. Charleen was setting the table. She motioned for Sarah to come and sit down. Sarah sat down in front of a large bowl of chili, a generous strip of garlic bread, and a half plate of vegetables.

"So, tell me, what did your friends think about the tower?"

"They loved it!"

"And what about you?"

"I thought it was fun. It's very high tech, that's for sure."

"Ya thinkin' about stickin' around for a while?"

"Looks that way. Pete needs me to stay for the next three months to train his staff on proper electrical maintenance. What about you? Are you still cooking for anyone?"

Charleen shook her head. "Nope. It seems that Pete doesn't need me to cook anymore."

"That's a shame. You'd be perfect for that Mars restaurant, the Red Planet Rotation."

"You think so? I'd give anything to be a chef there."

Sarah pulled out her cell phone and dialed a number. A gruff voice answered. "Yeah, who's there?"

"It's Sarah."

"Yeah? What do ya want?" Pete said in the middle of a bite.

"I'm sorry, Mr. Mayor. Did I catch you while you are eating?"

"Yes! Now what do you want?"

"I'm guessing that's room service. How does it taste?"

"Adequate. Now please, get to the point!"

"How would you like some good food again? How about making Charleen the head chef over at the Red Planet Rotation?"

Suddenly there erupted choking noises on the other end of the phone, then the sound of Pete coughing up some food. "What?" he replied in the midst of coughs. "She wants to cook at the Rotation?"

"Yes, that's right."

"Excellent! Tell her she's hired! I was hoping she'd want to cook again. Show up tomorrow at seven o'clock with her in uniform, and she can have the job."

"I'll let her know."

"Good. See you tomorrow. Bye." Sarah closed the phone.

"What did he say?"

A big grin formed on Sarah's face. "You're hired!" The girls squealed with glee.

"Wow! Sarah, I don't know how to thank you."

"It's nothing. You just need to catch him at the right time."

Once they were done with supper, Charleen joined Sarah at the tower for some shootin' fun. They didn't stay long; they needed a good night's sleep for the day ahead.

Chapter 14

Six-forty-five the next morning found Sarah waiting in the hotel lobby. Charleen came running out of the elevator clutching a compact in one hand and a powder brush in the other. "Sorry, I'm a little behind. I had to make sure my uniform was ready. Here, I've got a little breakfast for ya." She took a small plastic bag hanging from her wrist and handed it to Sarah.

Sarah pulled a small container of fruit and a thermos from the bag.

"That's orange juice in the thermos."

"Thank you, Charleen."

"Don't mention it. Now let's git on over to the tower!"

Dogleg Pete stood waiting at the top of the tower steps in front of the entrance. "Good morning," he greeted them, "you both look nicely dressed." They both wore their Mars Occurrence Tower uniform.

"Good morning," replied both ladies.

"Charleen, welcome on board. I look forward to eating your cooking again. If you will take the staff elevator to the Mars Base Camp, your crew is waiting for you at the Rotation."

They entered the tower and passed through a staff door that was to the right of the launch pods. They walked down a short corridor and passed an elevator. This is where Charleen stopped.

"Come see me around twelve-thirty. I'll have something special for ya for lunch."

"I'll be there," answered the gruff voice.

"Not you, Pete, Sarah."

The girls laughed. "Ok, I'll be there."

Pete led Sarah to the far end of the space station to the same room he had taken her to before. There stood five men. Each one looked like they could rip the place apart. Each one also looked like they did not want to be there. That changed when Sarah walked in.

"This is your crew," said Pete. He went through their names. Sarah knew it was going to be days before she remembered them. "Boys, behave. Sarah, take it away." Pete left.

Sarah eyed each one, all Thuderdykes, wondering how to begin. She spotted an instrument on a nearby desk. She grabbed it and held it up. "Can someone tell me what this is?"

"That's the thing you use to measure electrical stuff," answered short, bald man in a stupid voice. The men laughed.

Then a tall man on the end said, "That's an Ohm meter."

"Good," replied Sarah. *This is not going to be easy,* Sarah thought to herself. She began to pace in front of them. "Ok, men, at ease. For some of you, this is going to be easy. For others," she eyed the short, bald man, "it's going to take a while." As she was stopped in front of the tall man on the end, she felt a hand approach her backside. She smiled and shoved the end of her shotgun into his stomach. "But don't try to mess around, or you'll regret it!"

Sarah had to get out of there. She spotted five brand new textbooks. She picked up each one and handed them to the men. "Here, study these until I get back." Sarah then walked out of the room.

Sarah headed to the end of level one and the entrance of level two. She was halfway when a holographic zombie jumped out at her. As she fired at it, she noticed that it flickered. After it disappeared, she walked over to the wall and pulled off the covering. The emitter was blinking as well.

She called up the control room. "Ok, men, I need someone to the utility area. We've got a flickering holographic emitter."

Sarah hung up and began to examine the emitter. As she was doing this, she felt two hands on her sides. Sarah was not going to have this. She swung around and put the barrel of her shotgun in the man's chest. "You better be thankful this isn't a real gun."

He laughed. "Just thought we'd enjoy some alone time."

"The only alone time you are going to get is after work and not with me. From now on, you guys work in groups! Now, do you know how to fix this?"

"Yeah."

"Then, fix it! I'm heading on to level two."

Sarah left and took the hidden ladder to the second level.

After five more broken emitters, three of which she was able to fix herself, and two of which she had to call the men in to fix, she was glad when lunch time came. She found Charleen sitting alone at one of the tables with two plates of the most delicious pancakes that she had ever seen. Each plate held three large pancakes that were lightly buttered and covered with a heavy strawberry syrup.

"Hey, Sarah! How was yer morning?"

"Long! How's cooking?"

"It's great! I made these just for us."

"They look delicious! Pancakes for lunch?"

"Why not? I think it would be a hit, don't you?"

"I would give it a try if I were you."

This is how Sarah's days went for the next month and a half. She would patrol the tower looking for malfunctioning electrical equipment and report them to her team.

It was at the end of one day that the mayor called a meeting with all the staff. "I have some great news! A breakthrough has been made. In just two weeks, the reason for building this tower will be revealed, and you all will have front row seats! Also, everyone is allowed up to three guests. Make sure they can be here the entire day."

That night, Sarah called up Katie and Zammie.

"Girls, you need to come back here in two weeks! Pete's unveiling a breakthrough."

"Do you know what it is?"

"Nope. I haven't a clue."

"We'll be there. And we'll make sure Dexter comes along as well. I'm sure he'll want to see what the big surprise is too."

"Thank you, Katie."

"Oh, by the way, how's the job going?"

"It's ok. The guys on the team are a bunch of jerks! Everyone of them are either daydreaming about a date with me or daydreaming about being trapped inside the tower with hordes of zombies surrounded by a huge arsenal of fantastic weapons. It's been tough to keep their minds on what they are doing."

"I'm sure you can handle it. See you in two weeks."

The next two weeks passed with ease for Sarah. With her renewed excitement, she had no problems controlling her crew. Her early disciplinary actions sufficed to keep them in line and under control.

Sarah hugged her friends when she saw them in the lobby of the hotel. "Katie, Zammie, Dex, it's good to see you again. Thank you for taking time out of your busy schedules to come. I was beginning to go crazy."

They all laughed.

"We're here for you, Sarah, you know that," replied Zammie.

"I too am glad to see you again." Dexter took Sarah's hand.

"So am I," she replied, smiling up at him.

"So, when's this big surprise supposed to happen?"

"Sometime tomorrow."

"Good. That's a long drive up here, you know. It'll give us time to get some sleep."

"I see you all brought your shotguns." Sarah noticed the black straps over their shoulders.

"But of course! We couldn't miss a chance to take up some target practice."

Sarah didn't keep them for long. She could see that the trip had taken a lot out of them. Any catching up could be done the next day. "Be here at 7:30 sharp. I'm sure Charleen will have a wonderful breakfast for us."

Sarah was right. The four of them were shown to a special table near the windows with a breathtaking view of the Mars landscape.

Charleen personally came out to get their orders.

"Good morning, Sarah, what can I get for you and your friends?"

"Good morning, Charleen." Sarah turned to face the others. "Are pancakes ok for you all? Her pancakes are the best!" Everyone nodded. Sarah turned back to Charleen. "Then pancakes it is."

"Thank you, Dear. I'll bring out milk and juice for everyone. Oh, Sarah, Pete wants to meet with you after you are done. You can find him on the top floor in the west tower."

"Hmm, I wonder what he wants. Thank you, Charleen, I'll meet him after we eat."

"So, Sarah, are you trying to be secretive or do you really not know what the surprise is?" asked Dexter.

Sarah shook her head. "I'm sorry, Dex, but I really have no idea. Charleen doesn't know either. It looks like only certain members of his family know."

"Then this is really going to be interesting. And not to mention it's a little nerve racking. Knowing the mayor's background, I'm getting concerned. This tower

144

turned out great! That is a plus. But whatever he has planned could also turn out bad, very bad."

"Humph! Mr. Analytical!" commented Katie.

After a few minutes of debating over what the surprise could be, Charleen came back out with their food. She had four plates loaded with lightly buttered pancakes, only these did not have syrup already poured over them. Instead, she brought out three pitchers of thick syrup: one strawberry, one blueberry, and one maple.

"Giving us a choice?" asked Sarah.

"Sure thing! Thought it would help people like the pancakes better. What do ya think?"

"It's perfect," replied Dexter. "I think you've got a great idea."

"Charleen, it's simple, but it works," added Sarah.

"Thank you, guys!" she cheered and bounded back to the kitchen.

"She's quite energetic," Zammie said between bites of food.

"She loves to cook."

After most of the pancakes were gone and bites were few and far between, Sarah held up her shotgun. "Hey K, Z, are you ready? I've had time to build up five million points!"

"No fair, we've only gotten two and a half million points. We're going to have to do something about that!"

Katie and Zammie grabbed their guns and leapt from the table. Sarah wasn't going to be left behind, so she burst out after them. That left Dexter all alone at the table to pick up the bill, which he did with a chuckle.

After about half an hour later, Sarah realized that she was supposed to meet Pete right after breakfast. She hurried as fast as she could up to the west tower.

The room was empty. The seats were raised and the stage lit. "Pete, I'm here," called out Sarah.

Pete appeared out of nowhere beside the large, Martian stone device.

"Ah, Sarah, there you are. I was beginning to wonder if you got my message."

"Yes, I did. I'm sorry, I was chasing after some friends."

"Fine. Come on up here."

Sarah walked up onto the stage and turned to face Pete and the rest of the room. She noticed something that she had never seen before. From the stone device to the far wall stretched a black wall. Sarah walked out to the seats and turned to face the wall. She couldn't see it. All she could see was what looked like the stage.

She walked back onto the stage. "What's going on here, Pete?"

"Welcome to the biggest secret in this tower," replied Pete. He opened a trap door in the stage floor behind the wall. He pointed down at it and motioned for Sarah to approach. Sarah peered into the darkness and saw a small leather seat in a high tech cart. "It is how we travel from tower to tower." He then pointed to a bunch of large cables that ran from the stone device down through the trap door. "I need you to check these cables." He set a backpack down next to her. She opened it to find some pretty fancy meters.

"Ok."

Pete helped her down into the cart seat. "You should find a junction where you can hook up one of the meters." Sarah found it and was able to attach the first meter to the cables. "Good. Now lie back and touch the panel on the cart beside the seat." Sarah did as she was told and the panel lit up. "Use the arrow keys to move the cart. Go ahead down the tunnel and check the cables in the middle. I'll let you know when I need you to take the reading."

Sarah fiddled with the controls until the cart began to move down the tunnel. She got the cart to stop at the middle junction and attached the meter. "Are you ready?" came a shout from the other end.

"Yes, I'm ready here."

Sarah watched the meter. The power jumped, but the signal remained stable. Then a sudden wave of heat hit her in the face. She hit the control panel by accident causing the cart to race to the east end of the tunnel. Sarah then hooked up the meter to the cable junction on that side and studied the readout. The power level had decreased.

"How were the power levels?"

"A little high, but stable," answered Sarah.

"Good." Pete's voice sounded like it had come from that side of the tunnel, but he didn't come through the tunnel nor did he have enough time to go down through the tower to this side either. She dismissed the thought.

Sarah glanced back at the meter and saw the power jump again. She then felt the same wave of heat come from the center of the tunnel. She waited a few minutes before heading back through the tunnel on the cart. She examined the cables, looking for signs of damage due to the increase in power. But in spite of the mysterious heat, the cables appeared to be in perfect condition.

Pete helped Sarah out of the cart on the end where she started.

"Perfect. Everything looks to be in order. Go get your friends and bring them up. We are ready to get started."

Sarah called up Dexter and found Katie and Zammie on their way into the tower room in hopes of finding a horde of monsters to shoot. They were disappointed to find the room empty, but that disappointment was quickly forgotten when they discovered that the show was about to begin. Dexter soon followed, and the gang took their seats towards the front of the room. Within minutes, the room was full, and Pete stepped around the stone device and addressed the crowd.

"Ladies and gentlemen, welcome to the crowning event of this tower!" His voice boomed over the speaker systems in both towers. A dozen monitors around the room switched focus between the crowd in the other tower and Pete. "If you thought the teleporting device was amazing at the opening, just wait till you see it now. First, we need to dispel the illusion. Guys, lower the wall!"

To everyone's amazement, the entire right side of the stage went black and then began to descend into the floor. Although the right side of the stage appeared exactly the same as on the wall, no one had any clue that it was all fake, except Dexter.

"I knew it was all fake," whispered Dexter to Sarah and then to Katie and Zammie.

"Now, let's light up the device."

The bright blue barrier popped into existence in the middle of the stone device. Pete stepped up and walked right through it, although he didn't disappear; he passed right through like he was passing through curtains. He then walked straight over to the trap door in the stage floor and lifted it up. "Up until now, we have been using that tunnel as a way to get myself and the rest of my staff over to the other tower giving the illusion that we were really teleporting over there. Tonight, I will defy all logic and step through that device and emerge instantly on the other side in the other tower. Guys, light it up for real this time!"

The bright blue barrier vanished and a dark blue one appeared in its place. Pete walked around the device and walked through it, like before, only this time, he did not come out the other side. The audience drew their attention to the monitors which showed Pete in the other tower. The audience went wild.

"Thank you! Thank you!" The crowd got quiet. "And to prove this is real, I need someone from the audience. You!" Pete pointed to a young, dark skinned man. He was laughing with his friends, enjoying all of the tower hype until Pete pointed him out. He was now the focus of attention. "Come on up here."

The young man stood, straightened his apparel and walked up onto the stage and stood next to Pete. "How do you like the tower?"

"It's cool!" he said towards the audience and all his friends cheered. "You totally got it all right. I got six million points in one day!"

"That's good. Now I need your help to prove something to these people. Do you think your tough enough to handle it?"

"Yo, Dude, I'm tough!"

"Then step through that device." Pete pointed to the Martian stone device.

The young man took a couple steps back. "Now wait just a minute."

"What's wrong? You're not scared are you?"

He froze. The cheering died. Faint snickers began filling his ears. His face toughened. He stepped towards the device.

"Good decision. Go ahead and step through; I'll be right behind you."

The young man stepped through the device, instantly appearing in the other tower. Pete stepped through a few seconds afterwards. "See, that wasn't so difficult, was it?"

Cheering erupted from both towers as the young man danced around the stage.

In the middle of cheering, Sarah glanced up at Dexter. He was as white as a ghost. "Dexter, what's wrong?"

"He got it to work?" His voice was more of shock than amazement.

"It looks that way. Is that a bad thing?"

Dexter was silent for a minute. "Something's not right here."

Dexter remained silent for the rest of his stay at the tower. Katie and Zammie, however, talked up a storm with Sarah about how amazing this breakthrough was.

They tried admitting that Dexter had been right all along that the teleporting was all an illusion, but it didn't work.

"Well, girls, looks like everything is going great here for Pete. I'll be home in one month." Sarah hugged the girls, and they said their goodbyes. She tried to get Dexter to smile, but it didn't work.

"Don't worry about, Dex, Sarah. We'll get his spirits back up in no time."

Sarah smiled. "I know you will."

"Come on, Z, we've got to get back and get the mansion put back together." Katie poked Zammie in the side.

"Oh, yeah, that's right," replied Zammie.

"What!"

The girls laughed.

"Don't worry, Sarah, we're just joking. The mansion's still in one piece."

Sarah joined the laughter.

Chapter 15

For the next two weeks, business was booming at the tower. Reporters, TV crews, and not to mention all the guests showing up, filling the hotels! Sarah could barely keep up with the electrical maintenance. It was a good thing that her crew learned from her instruction and started working as a team.

The teleportation shows were packed. At least two or three audience members per show went with the staff member, who was leading the show, through the stone device. This action seemed to solidify the fact that the teleportation was real.

Then reports started coming in about people, all over the country, who started seeing strange marks appear on their bodies. Even the staff members started wearing long, hooded robes to hide the marks that were appearing on their bodies. Sarah was the only staff member who did not show signs of these strange marks, but then again, Sarah was the only staff member who had not gone through the Martian teleportation device.

Friday night came. The tower closed early that night to prepare for the following day. Dogleg Pete had ordered that the tower be closed for the entire day on Saturday because he felt that Sarah should make a full inspection of the place with her team before she retired as their Electrical Specialist.

After an early supper, Sarah joined Charleen in her hotel suite for some coffee.

"Charleen, before everything winds to a close tomorrow for me, I wanted ask you something. Do you know how the lottery got started?"

"Dear, that is a very strange and mysterious story; are ya sure you want to hear it?"

Sarah nodded.

"Well then, it stared hundreds of years ago when a young farmer stumbled across that wooded area that would later become Whachmikilu. He cut down some of them trees there and built a small cabin."

"Was he a Thuderdyke?"

Charleen shook her head. "Nope, but don't worry, we'll come into the story later.

"Now, we're not quite sure why he built that cabin or what exactly he built it fer, but we do know that he visited the cabin so much that be built a road right to its very front doorstep. He called it Dead End Cabin.

"Years went by, and he got married and moved himself and his wife into that cabin. They had children and cleared out much of the center of that wooded area and built other cabins for his kids to have as their own.

"When the children were old enough and began living on their own in those cabins, they started building shops and businesses from which to sustain a proper village. Everything went along smoothly until the fiftieth anniversary of that first cabin being built. The children all gathered with their families to celebrate when they found a horrific sight. The inside of the cabin was covered with strange stones, candles, and blood. Their parents had been murdered and no one knew how."

"That's scary. What did they do?"

"The children tore down the cabin and built a large meeting house in its place." Charleen saw Sarah's eyes widen. "Yes, it's that same meeting house.

"The meeting house became the center of the village, and the village began to grow. Some have even said that the ghost of the farmer put a curse on the place preventing those who moved in from ever leaving. I tell ya, there was always this creepy feeling in my bones when living there. I can still feel it today, although it's not as strong.

"The village back then was known as Dead End.

"Now we come into the picture. We were immigrants from across the sea. We came to this country to begin a new life.

"I'm sure you're curious about how we got our name. Well, it wasn't always Thuderdyke. We got that name because of our trade back then. 'Dyke' came from the dykes we built and 'thuder' from the odd sort of thud our tools made when they struck wood.

"Anyways, it was Jedediah Thuderdyke I who came across the small village of Dead End. I'm not sure what he was thinking, but he loved the place... so much that he moved the entire Thuderdyke family into the village. He talked to everyone he came across about the village's mysterious past. Some of the original children were still alive, although they were now very old.

"He was the talk of the village. They were so brainwashed by him that no one batted an eye when he started the lottery."

Sarah's jaw dropped. "Why would he do such a thing?"

"Population control. At least that's what the official story was. So many people in one spot with the irresistible desire to never leave the village was a good cover story. The unofficial story was that it was power and a control like we had never had before. The village was renamed to Whachmikilu and Jedediah was voted the first mayor of the village. He rigged the lottery so that no Thuderdyke family ever won."

"Ok, that explains a lot. What about Pete and this crazy notion to build a super tower theme park?"

"Well, until Pete came along, all of the mayors of the village were Thuderdykes. This way, we could remain in control of life itself in the village. We always wanted something grand to work towards, but we never knew what that would be. When Pete came along, we knew we had found our man to lead us to something wondrous, so we made him the first non-Thuderdyke mayor of the village.

"As for this place, here's where it gets confusing. We knew that we would someday do something great, but we never settled on anything specific until a few years after Pete became mayor. He just announced one day to the family that he had found these magnificent stone devices that now sit in the top of the towers.

"Some say that we launched a secret mission to Mars and found the two stones; others say that Pete found the devices in the mountains that surrounded the village. The artifacts in the research labs are real, although I'm not sure where they came from. Some have told me they come from Mars and were really part of the ancient Martian culture. Others tell me they come from the same caverns where Pete found the two devices, in the mountains around the village."

"What do you think about all this?"

"Well, please don't go tellin' Pete that I told ya any of this, but I think the family has jumped off the deep end, if ya know what I mean." Sarah nodded. "I mean this tower is nice and all, but the end doesn't justify the means." There were a few minutes of silence then Charleen thrust out her hand towards Sarah. "I did get this!"

On the ring finger of Charleen's left hand sat a large diamond on a gold band. "Josh asked me to marry him!"

A large smile jumped onto Sarah's face as she grasped her friend's hand. "Congratulations! But wait, aren't you both... well... the same family?"

"Yeah, but extremely distant. His great grandmother is the sister of my great aunt, so it's all good. Now I've told ya about my family, what about yours?"

Sarah tried to say something, but her words got caught in a very large yawn.

"Oh, my! Now look what I've gone and done. Tomorrow is going to be a very important day for ya, and I've gone on yackin' and yackin' totally forgettin' that you need sleep. Now run on up to your room and git some!

We can talk more about your family over lunch tomorrow."

As Sarah got up to leave, she grinned over at Charleen. "Now you get some sleep too."

"Can't," she replied back to Sarah's surprise. "Josh has to work late at the tower, and I told him I would make him a midnight snack at the Rotation."

Sarah nodded, left the room and took the elevator to her floor. Once in her room, she took a long, hot shower before going to bed. As sleep began to overtake her, she couldn't stop wondering if something was about to happen. She had seen the strange marking on Charleen's hand when she showed her the ring, but Sarah had decided not to say anything. What was it? What did it mean? Was it a warning to stop what they were doing or statement of inescapable doom? Sarah was glad she would be leaving this place and told herself it would be for a very long time.

Chapter 16

Suddenly, Sarah's sleep was interrupted by a phone ringing. She picked it up.

"Sarah, something's gone wrong, we need you in the tower control room right away!"

"Josh?" Sarah recognized the voice.

"Yeah, it's me." He coughed. "Get here as quickly as you can."

Sarah glanced over at the clock. Midnight. "Ok, I'll be there."

She hung up the phone and threw on her black uniform.

She hurried to the elevator and pulled out her cell phone. She dialed the number for her mansion back in Eagle Point. A half awake Zammie answered.

"Zammie, it's Sarah."

Zammie yawned. "Oh hi, Sarah, how are you?"

"Zammie, something's gone wrong. I'm going to need your and Katie's help."

Zammie instantly woke up upon hearing those words. "Ok. What happened? What do you need us to do?"

"At this point, I'm not sure what happened. I got a call from Josh saying that something went wrong and about getting over to the tower as quickly as possible. With the strange marks appearing on everyone, I'm not taking any chances." Sarah was now out of the elevator and running across the lobby. "I need you to contact Chopper and get here as fast as you can."

"Sure. Where do you want us to pick you up?"

"One of the towers. Land on the one with the landing lights on."

She then rushed out of the hotel, over to the tower, through the entrance and the staff halfway, and through the space station. As she neared the door to the control room, she heard loud banging.

She opened the door to find two staff members hitting some computer equipment with long, metal pipes. "Hey, what do you think you are doing?" she shouted. They didn't stop.

"Here, you might need these." The voice came from a man who sat slumped against the wall. He tossed two fully loaded pistols to her. When she paused, looking puzzled, he pleaded with her further. "Quickly, before they destroy that computer!"

Sarah warned the two again before firing a round into each of their upper torsos. They turned to face her. It wasn't the strange Martian symbols scared into their faces that repulsed her; it was the fact that it appeared that their mouths had been ripped apart by some unnatural force. She gasped at the sight of them as they approached her.

She emptied each pistol into them, and they fell twitching to the floor.

Sarah turned to face the man whom she now recognized as Josh Thuderdyke.

"Josh, what's going on?"

"Sarah, you must stop Pete!" he replied.

"Why? What happened?"

"He should have never attempted the teleportation. Just like in the game, it did not go as planned. Whoever goes through eventually turns into a mindless zombie. But before that happens, symbols appear on their bodies." He pointed out the symbols that had appeared on his face and arms.

"Do you have any idea what they are?"

"Yes, we do. They are the symbols of the Martian language."

"What do they say?"

"They say, 'Beware, the Devil cometh.' Creepy, huh?"

"Yeah." A chill ran up Sarah's spine. "What should I do?"

Josh began to cough. He put a cloth handkerchief to his mouth until his coughs went away. When he lowered it, Sarah saw blood.

"Are you ok?"

"My transformation has begun. There's nothing anyone can do about it now." He took one of the pistols from Sarah and reloaded it. He handed it back to her. "The first thing you must do is shoot me. Put me out of my misery before I become like them." He handed her his access card. "Second, you must find the hidden panel that is just outside this room. I am the weapons specialist. I

160

have access to panels that no one else knows about. Inside them are live weapons with ammo. Use them to stay alive and find Pete."

"Are you sure there are no alternatives? I could get you to a hospital."

"We've already tried. Nothing works against this." Sarah was silent. She then gave Josh a grin. "Before I forget, congratulations. I saw the ring you gave Charleen." Josh didn't smile. In fact, he began to turn white. "Josh, what happened?" Sarah's mind immediately thought of the strange mark she had seen on Charleen's hand.

Josh shook his head. "You don't want to know."

"Where is she? I was just with her a few hours ago. I need to see her!"

"I'm sorry, Sarah, but that isn't possible."

"What? Why?" Sarah was getting agitated.

"Trust me, you don't want to know." He began to cough again, followed by moaning. "Hurry, Sarah, it's happening!"

Sarah stood, but she hesitated. After more pleading, Sarah raised the gun, closed her eyes, and fired.

She ran from the room clutching the pistol in one hand and the access card in the other. As she slammed into the wall opposite the door, a panel slid to the side. She peered inside to find a shotgun and a fanny pack filled with shotgun shells.

Sarah placed the pistol inside and grabbed the fanny pack and put in around her waist. She then grabbed the shotgun and checked to see if it was loaded. It was. She then slowly walked down the corridor.

"Can anyone hear me?" came a gruff voice over the tower intercom. It was the voice of Dogleg Pete.

"Yes, I can hear you," Sarah said back.

"Ah, Sarah. I need your help. The staff have locked me in the show room in the west tower. Get up here as soon as you can."

"I'll try," she replied back.

Suddenly, a hooded figured jumped out in front of her.

"Ah, fresh meat," growled the man under the hood.

"Stay back, I'm warning you!"

The hooded man did not stop. Sarah fired. The hooded man flew backwards and lay twitching on the floor. Sarah hurried past.

The rest of the corridor to the far junction was silent. The simulated view of the outside of the space station to her right and left gave Sarah an eerie feeling. She kept glancing from left to right and around behind her, making sure that no one leapt out from beneath the walkway.

When she neared the junction, she hid just inside the doorway. She peered out into the large room and saw a group of hooded staff huddled to one side. She saw her intended destination, two doors leading to the locker room. She pocketed Josh's access card and pulled out hers. She then readied her shotgun just in case she needed it and prepared to run.

Sarah then dashed out from her hiding spot and ran as a fast as she could to the locker room doors. She could hear the shouts of the staff members as they saw her run past. "Look! It's Dr. Mitchell! Get her!"

She swiped her card and burst through the doors. She then swiped her card on the other side and entered a lock code that Charleen had told her about shortly after becoming the head chef at the Rotation. The hooded staff members were now at the door attempting to break it open. Sarah realized that someone might have an access key of their own. She looked around and saw a short, metal pipe. She grabbed it and shoved it through the handles of the doors. "That should hold them."

Sarah opened her locker and pulled out the large duffel bag. She then turned to the doors to the room, winked at the mad crowd trying to get in, and disappeared around the corner into the changing room. Sarah turned on the lights and walked around the room, making sure it was empty. It was.

Sarah undressed, opened the duffel bag, pulled out her suit, stepped into it, and zipped up the back. She put on the boots and locked them into place. She then slipped on the gloves and locked them onto the sleeves. After bunching up her hair, she placed the helmet over her head and locked it. Last but not least, Sarah slid her arm inside the beautiful, golden cannon. It clicked into place and started to glow. She flipped through the modes with a grin on her face.

Once everything was in place and functioning, Sarah became a different person. No longer was she Dr. Sarah Mitchell, Electrical Specialist; she was Miss Doom. She now had a cause, a reason to bring judgment on those who had caused so much death and chaos, not to mention those who had killed her own father.

Transformed into hopeless zombies by the Mars teleportation device, the Thuderdyke clan had no hopes of recovery. Josh had left Sarah with no other choice but to shoot him and the other two Thuderdykes in the room. She felt the same fate was due to the others as well.

Sarah stepped out of the changing room and faced the doors. The crowd of mad staff members was still trying to break down the doors, with no success.

"Hey, look!" called out one of them, "I guess we'd better prepare to be judged!" They all laughed.

Sarah chuckled. "I'd stand back if I were you."

Sarah fired a couple rounds at the door; the cannon glowed blue. After the doors were a nice frosty white, she stopped firing and changed the cannon color to red. She smiled. "Ok, boys, the party's over." Sarah began to run towards the doors. When she was halfway across the room, she began firing, repeatedly at the doors. They burst into fragments sending those standing close to them down to the floor.

As Sarah ran, she continued to fire into the crowd, creating a pathway through them. Those, who were fortunate enough to only be hit with a single blast, fell to the ground, severely burned. Those, who were hit more than once, well, caused quite a mess. Once she had passed through the crowd, Sarah did not turn to see if any of them had decided to pursue her; she just kept running towards the center of the space station.

Once at the center, Sarah slipped through the heavy, black curtains. She used the glow of the cannon to find her way to a ladder leading upwards. At the top, Sarah peered out from between the curtains. She spotted a group of staff members fighting over something. Sarah got the idea that maybe there was someone trapped by the group and fired three blasts into the crowd sending three members to the floor. Her action did not have the intended effect of luring them away. Instead, to her horror, they turned their attention to the fallen bodies. Sarah had no desire to stick around and watch, so she bolted from the curtains and through the door to the Mars Base Camp.

Once inside, she spotted the sign pointing the way to the food area. She thought of Charleen and determined that she just had to know. When she got to the restaurant, she screamed and turned away. Lying on the floor just inside the entrance was a severed arm. Sarah recognized the ring as one that Charleen had just showed her. A tear ran down Sarah's cheek.

She ran back down the corridor and into the utility facility and was surprised when no one leapt out. Reaching for the lever to open up the way to level two, she was grabbed from behind and hurled across the floor.

In the dim light, Sarah saw a strange sight. What looked like a man's torso sat on top of a motorized wheelchair. The chair was quick and appeared to respond to the man's thoughts like the chair was his legs. She attempted to hit the man with the different modes of her cannon. Each attempt missed; they were too slow.

An idea then came to her. She fired a purple ball of arching energy at the man. She missed but came close enough to cause the desired effect. The wheelchair began to jerk and stall. Sarah continued to fire, hitting the chair a couple times until it became completely unresponsive.

Sarah quickly put the deformed Thuderdyke out of his misery, flipped the switch, and hurried through the open panel door and up the ladder to level two.

Sarah found the glass walls to the research rooms broken. Deranged staff members threw artifacts across the room at each other. When they saw Sarah, she became the target.

Sarah dodged the artifacts and fought back. When she had taken care of those in that room, she proceeded down the adjacent corridor towards the elevator to level three. She didn't make it very far, though, for more doomed staff members attacked her from the research rooms as she passed by.

Distracted by the fighting, Sarah lost her way a total of five times before finding the elevator she had been looking for. She guessed that she had been on that level for at least an hour if not more.

Sarah knew that the third level was going to be tricky. This level was a complete maze. Sarah was tired from the previous levels, so she was glad when not many staff members stepped out into her path. The lack of many opponents also helped keep her on track as to which direction was the right one to take. It took her a little over half an hour to find the hidden elevator to the top of the west tower, but she was thankful when she did find it.

At the top, she discovered the room to be almost pitch black. "Mayor, it's Sarah. Where are you?" Sarah saw movement on the stage. "Dogleg, is that you?"

A laughter erupted from the figure on the stage as machine gun bullets began shooting past Sarah. She dived behind the last row of seats. She didn't know if the suit was bulletproof.

"Pete's in the other tower. I came up here to show him my new arms. I guess he didn't take it too well and teleported to the other side." The figure fired again.

Sarah waited for a pause in the barrage of bullets before taking aim and firing a barrage of her own. The figure continued to fire and laugh. "Give up, Sarah; I'm getting hungry!" Sarah endured the brief nauseating feeling and fired back.

Then, the sound of the figure's guns jamming reached Sarah's ears. She took her chance and stood up to get a better aim and fired. The figure was blown back across the stage into a heap against the wall.

"Good work, Sarah," came Pete's gruff voice over the speaker system. "Come on over to the east tower and we'll talk." The stone device popped into life with its dark, blue barrier in the center.

Sarah hesitated, not wanting to become like the other members of the Thuderdyke clan. She then remembered the tunnel cart and the hidden trap door. She quickly opened the door and climbed down into the cart. She operated the controls and whisked herself through the tunnel and over to the other tower. She silently opened the trap door on that side and climbed out. She was glad to find Pete's back to her as he studied the computer screens. She waited till she had stepped in front of the stone device before speaking.

"It's over, Mayor. You've got nowhere else to go."

He turned around and said with a grin, "Why Sarah, whatever do you mean?"

"Your tower was a great idea; you should have stopped there, but you went further and attempted the impossible. The result was an immoral mess!"

"That's what you think. Tell me, Sarah, what was your father's name?"

Sarah smiled. "Dr. Kyle Smith was his name."

Pete began a low chuckle. "Then it really is hell."

"What?"

"Kyle Smith's baby died. She was drug off by some wild animals at his final Lottery. When you passed through that device, you picked up her soul, and now she wants revenge for killing her and her family."

"You're only half correct, Pete! The Smith's baby did die, but not at the Lottery; she died in the nursery just after birth. Dr. Smith switched babies with my mother, Abby. Mom knew that I would have a good home with the Smiths, so she only pretended to grieve. At the Lottery, she found me and made it look like I had been drug away by wild animals."

"Brilliant! No wonder she wanted to leave the village so quickly. By the way, nice suit. I'm sorry that it's not going to help you out of your personal nightmare that you have just stepped into."

"That's where you are wrong again. I did not go through the device like you hoped." She pointed to the trap door in the stage floor which was still open. "I went through there."

Pete yelled in rage and ran towards Sarah. Sarah fired, sending Pete flying backwards hard against the computer terminals. His mechanical suit he wore protected his body against the initial blast, but his head hit pretty hard against the side of one of the terminals.

Sarah approached Pete, who looked dazed. He held out his hand. "Don't come any closer."

"What's going on, Pete?"

"You're right. We are no closer to getting this technology to work than the Martians. We should have heeded their warnings." Pete's face twisted and contorted like he was in tremendous pain. "Sarah, you must get out of here! But first, know this; no matter who they possess; no matter what artifacts they create or destroy; they will never be able to escape from their prison."

"Is there any hope for those who have been affected by the device?"

Pete shook his head. He then reached up onto the computer terminal and handed Sarah a computer disk. "No. At least we couldn't find any. This contains all the research done on the Martian culture and the devices."

Sarah didn't have any pockets in her suit, so she picked up a roll of duct tape that was sitting nearby and taped the disk, in its case, to the side of her suit. She turned back to the mayor, who was convulsing very strongly. She stood and backed away, aiming her cannon at him.

"Go ahead, before it's too late!" he yelled.

Sarah began to fire multiple rounds into Pete. Instead of exploding like the others had done, Pete's skin began to crack and break apart. A red, muscle-like mass began to expand from his body. Pete turned into a large, red, demonic looking creature with two large, brown horns gauging from his head.

Sarah continued to fire at the creature, which rubbed the blast spots and grinned. "Ah, warm and refreshing," grunted the creature. A large fireball appeared in the creature's hand. He threw it at Sarah. She dodged just in time.

Sarah switched the cannon to purple. "Hmm, maybe this will do something." She fired and hit the creature with a few shots. After dodging two more fireballs, she determined that this mode had no effect. She switched the color to yellow. Again, the blasts had no effect.

She switched the cannon to the final color, blue. She let go a single shot at the massive, red body. The creature scratched at the impact spot with his free hand while continuing to hurl fireballs with the other. "That's interesting," she mumbled to herself and let go two more shots.

This time, the creature used both hands to scratch his stomach. Sarah saw a chance and took it. She began to fire continuously with the blue mode. After twenty or thirty shots, the creature appeared to be in a frozen state. Sarah didn't waste time. She quickly changed the mode to red and fired at the center of the creature's torso. It exploded, sending hundreds of frozen red chunks showering around her.

Sarah collapsed in a seat in the front row. Her task was complete. She had stopped Pete. All she had to do now was to get out of there. Sarah remembered that on the back wall was a secret panel leading to a ladder that provided access to the roof. She found it after a little searching and climbed up. She had checked the landing lights once before, so finding the switch to turn them on again wasn't hard at all.

A gentle rain was falling outside. Sarah let it wash her suit clean of the mess she had picked up while fighting inside the tower. Once she was clean, she sat down near the ladder. She could feel the best friends' necklace under her suit, against her skin. She smiled and fell asleep. She knew her friends were on their way.

Hours later, Sarah awoke when someone shook her. It was Katie.

"Sarah, we're here, let's go!"

Sarah stood and followed Katie to the helicopter. She got in and removed her helmet.

"So, what happened?" asked Zammie.

Sarah told them what had taken place after her call to Zammie.

"Wow, what a nightmare!" commented Katie.

"Yeah," added Zammie, "good thing it's over."

Sarah pulled the disk from her side and handed it to Katie. "Here's all the research they collected on the Martian artifacts and those teleportation devices."

"Thank you. I'm sure someone will want to study that."

Sarah nodded but didn't say anything else. Although the girls had a million questions, they could see that Sarah was exhausted. They decided to be quiet the rest of the trip back to the mansion.

When they got back, Sarah took a shower and went straight to bed.

Chapter 17

It was pitch black. Sparks danced in the air every few seconds or so. An occasional light flickered illuminating a room or corridor. Small chunks of flesh fell from the ceiling and inched their way across the floor. A shadow moved in the west tower. "Sarah?" called the figure, "Sarah, are you here?"

A faint noise came from somewhere in the room.

"Sarah, where are you?"

The noise grew louder, echoing from somewhere in the distance. "No..."

The figure turned towards the direction of the sound. The dark blue barrier appeared suddenly in the center of the stone device.

"Sarah, are you in there?" the figure asked.

He heard the voice again, clearly coming from the center of the device. "No, don't!"

"Hold on, I'm coming!" The figure leaped into the barrier and disappeared.

"No!"

Sarah awoke at the sound of her own scream. She sat up in her bed. A cold sweat was dripping from her face. She wondered if what she just saw was real. She wondered if any of what had taken place the past year was real. Then she looked down next to her bed and saw the cannon.

She picked up the cannon and slipped her arm inside. The cannon began to glow. Sarah stared at it for a few seconds in disbelief. If the cannon was real, could the dream she just had be real as well? Sarah knew that there was only one way to find out...

The End.

Brent Harris
and son, Toby

Thank you for purchasing Sarah's Lottery. I hope you enjoyed the story.

I have been writing stories since high school; this is the first one to be published. I have many more stories that could, one day, be published.

Imagine you are a submarine captain, and your dream is to make your sub fly, but your first officer doesn't agree. You fire your first officer and hire an old flame to make your dream come true. On the eve of your first flight, the equipment malfunctions, sending you and your crew into the future where you find that your first officer and a foreign power have taken over your homeland. Can you figure out what went wrong and go back and correct history?

How about a famous painter with mysophobia? He lives on the third floor of a hotel and cannot use anything more than once. He is set in his routine, and it's a strange one. But what happens when his routine is suddenly changed? Can he hold it together long enough to put it back? Does it really go back to the way it was?

Contact: SarLot65@gmail.com

19130681R00098

Made in the USA
Charleston, SC
08 May 2013